EAGLE OF NIAGARA

For Teddy.

Hope you enjoy it.

Aunt Hazel.

BY JOHN BRICK

EAGLE
OF
NIAGARA

THE STORY OF DAVID HARPER AND HIS
INDIAN CAPTIVITY

CAVALCADE
BOOKS

DOUBLEDAY & COMPANY, INC., GARDEN CITY, NEW YORK, 1955

With the exception of actual historical personages identified as such, the characters are entirely the product of the author's imagination and have no relation to any person or event in real life.

LIBRARY OF CONGRESS CATALOG CARD NUMBER 55-5578

EAGLE OF NIAGARA

CHAPTER ONE

It was a cold, gray day. The bitter March wind rattled the bare limbs of the trees. Blowing in erratic gusts, it slashed the men's faces and probed into the folds of their clothing. Above the clearing, slate-gray clouds swept endlessly across the open patch of sky. Occasionally one of the men would lift his head and stare at the clouds, as if looking for the snow that usually came on a northeast wind.

David Harper shivered as a gust of wind more violent than most swept across the clearing. Resting his musket in the crook of his arm, he pulled the collar of his Canadian blanket coat higher. The coat was wearing thin. He would need a new one next winter. It would be the kind with a drawstring hood, if the quartermaster could get them. A man could stand a lot of weather if his neck and ears were protected. Dave was used to the long, cold Mohawk Valley winters, but he would be glad when this one was over. The soldiers in the Continental regiments of Washington's regular army were required to be out in weather that would drive wolves to shelter. Dave remembered the days before he'd enlisted in the Continental line, when he'd been a member of the Tryon County militia, stationed at the fort in Cherry Valley. In those days, snow, rain, or sleet kept the militia indoors by the fires. Life in the regular army was not so easy.

Dave looked enviously at the woodcutters, whose work was keeping them warm. There were a dozen of them sawing felled maple trees and splitting them into four-foot lengths. Dave regretted drawing the guard detail. With his lithe muscles and long experience in handling an ax, the woodcutting would be no great chore for him. As it was, however, he and the other six guards had to stand and freeze, while the woodcutters, warmed by their work, suffered only the discomfort of the biting wind in their faces.

Briefly Dave wondered if he should walk over and offer to spell one of the woodcutters. He discarded the idea, however. Corporal Betts might get angry, and if the corporal's temper was stirred, Dave was apt to end up on the wood detail for a week. Dave didn't want that duty. There was a hunting party due to leave the fort during the next couple of days, and Dave wanted to go with it.

Betts and the other five guards stood around a roaring fire they had built in the center of the clearing. Nearby, another fire burned. This one was much smaller, being fed with the chips hewn by the woodcutters' double-bitted axes. A great iron kettle hung over it, suspended by a chain from a tripod of maple poles. Now and then one of the guards turned away from the conversation at the larger fire to toss a few handfuls of chips on the cooking fire, or to stir the stew that bubbled in the kettle.

Dave wished that Betts would give the call to eat. He was almighty tired of salt beef stewed with turnips after a long winter in which that combination had almost always formed the main item of the garrison's daily diet, but this weather made a man hungry. He'd be glad to get a panful of that stew.

He permitted his mind to picture a big venison steak surrounded by onions and fresh greens and hot corn bread. He would give a year's pay for such a meal. A faint grin touched his lips. A year's pay wasn't much of a price. In the Continental Army in the late winter of 1781, a man hadn't much use for the paper money that the paymaster handed out in bundles tied with cord. Dave had seen many a soldier light his pipe with Continental currency. Congress and the states issued so much of it that it was almost worthless.

It seemed to Dave, as he thought of the hot meal ahead and watched Betts and the others warm themselves at the fire, that the wind had strengthened and grown colder. He looked around the clearing. The woodcutters had one sled loaded and were starting on the other. Probably Betts would call the men to eat when the second sled was ready.

He was sure that Betts and the rest considered him a fool for standing guard when he might huddle at the fire. The winter wasn't over by a long shot, and the Indians and John Butler's Rangers wouldn't be raiding in such weather. Winter had meant safety to the people of the Mohawk Valley ever since the war had started. The raiders stayed in their wilderness headquarters at Niagara from fall until spring. At Fort Stanwix, where Dave was stationed, the regulars relaxed when snow fell and drifted high in the woods, and took it easy until the warm winds of spring opened the trails from Niagara. However, Dave couldn't relax, no matter how foolish Betts and the others thought him. He kept remembering his father's tales of the old French War, and his advice about Indians.

"Remember this, Davey," he had said time and again. "Just when you think you're safe, they'll jump you. We never saw an Injun when we were looking for 'em, but as soon as we'd make up our minds there wasn't a hostile for fifty miles around, they'd be on us, yelling like devils. When you're out against 'em, you can't ever take it easy."

To help himself keep warm, Dave started a circuit of the clearing. He had to take off his snowshoes, because maple logs lay every which way in the drifted snow. The two yoke of oxen stood patiently in the packed snow of the trail, facing in the direction of Fort Stanwix, two miles away. The grinding movement of their lower jaws as they chewed their cuds was their only movement as they waited with placid dignity for the shouted "Geddup" and the touch of the goad that would send them surging into the yokes while the sleds behind them lurched into motion. Dave had the frontier farmer's love for fine oxen. These four were lean, slat-ribbed beasts, so undersized that any good farmer would turn up his nose at them, but they were the best the army could provide. In spite of their ugliness and the crusted dirt in their long winter coats, Dave was touched with affection for them. They reminded him of home, even though his father wouldn't have had such scrawny brutes on his farm.

The memory of his father and the happy days before the war came back sharply, as it always did when he least expected it. Bitterly he remembered the cold gray November day in 1778 when the Indians and Butler's Rangers had struck Cherry Valley in the midst of a driving storm, bringing fire and death to the beautiful settlement isolated among the hills south of the Mohawk River. With only a few minutes' warning, Nat Harper had seen his wife and three sons on their way to safety through the forest north of the valley, then had turned back toward the fort to join its defenders, though there was little hope that he would get through the ring of Rangers and Indians that encircled it.

Dave had wanted to go with his father, but he was entrusted with the care and safety of his mother and the two younger boys. He had watched his father slip away through the trees toward the wild whooping and the rattle of musketry in the center of the valley. Nat Harper and many other brave settlers met death that day at the hands of Joseph Brant's warriors and Butler's fierce woodsmen.

The day after the massacre, Dave had returned from the German Flats with Colonel Klock's militia. He had helped to bury his father with the other victims. Ever since, he had hated the enemy at Niagara, both the savage warriors led by the great Mohawk, Joseph Brant, and their white allies, the Rangers, led by Colonel John Butler and Captain Walter Butler, his son. He had joined the regular army to strike back at them, particularly at Brant, who had once been his father's friend in the old days of peace.

He shook off the memories—Cherry Valley had been raided three years ago. His bitterness had eased with the passage of time. He paused before the lead pair of oxen and scratched their rough heads. "It's not your fault you're so ugly," he said softly. "You do your best, don't you, boys?"

The oxen stopped chewing and stared at him with dull eyes. Dave smiled and moved toward the woodcutters.

"When's that stew goin' to be ready, Harper?" one of

the men called. "I could eat one of these here chunks of maple, happen I had some gravy to put on it."

"Soon, I guess," Dave said. "How many loads you going to haul today?"

"Six, if it don't snow," the man said. "Them fellers over to the fort ain't got no idea how much work it is to cut this stuff and haul it in. They burn big fires all the time and let the heat go up the chimney."

The man turned back to his work, still grumbling, and Dave passed by. Beyond the area where the men were working, the snow was unbroken, save for the scattered stumps that thrust ax-hewn points above the drifts. The erratic track of a rabbit was faintly etched into the smooth surface. Following it casually with his gaze, Dave saw where it ended abruptly beside a snow-covered log. The snow there was disturbed and dotted by flecks of blood. There was a tuft of grayish-brown fur clinging to a twig on the log.

As if he had witnessed the scene, Dave pictured what had happened. The foolish rabbit had come skipping across the snow in the moonlight, pausing every few yards to watch and listen for the danger that might lie anywhere around him. There had been no warning for him. The beat of heavy wings might have been the wind sighing in the trees; the shadow slipping across the snow might have been a cloud passing the face of the moon; the sibilance of the feathered body plummeting earthward might have been the noise of a snow-laden tree letting its burden fall. The owl struck with a thud, and instantly came the only sound the rabbit had ever uttered in its short life, its shrill death scream; finally, with a soft, rhythmic throbbing, the great wings carried the owl and its prey up into the darkness.

A man could learn all there was to know about the woods and its creatures by keeping his eyes and ears open. Here in the border country these past few years many a man had paid with his life for his inability to interpret the warnings of the wilderness.

Dave Harper was more capable than most young men in the art of woodsrunning. His father, before his farming days, had been a trapper and trader beyond the frontiers of New York and Pennsylvania. He had handed on to Dave most of his own great knowledge of the wilderness. Dave was tall and lean, with long sinewy legs. His face was darkened by the burning of wind and sun, and his hair was the same shining black as the inside of a walnut burr. His wide-set blue eyes were restless, always observing the land and the sky, picking out signs of game or weather changes that went unseen by his comrades. He seemed older and more mature than his twenty years. He walked around the clearing now with the silent, graceful stride of the woodsrunner, even in the heavy boots supplied by the regular army. He'd never had a pair of leather boots on his feet until he'd joined the army, and often, on the march, he wished that he could wear moccasins.

On his circuit of the clearing Dave saw nothing to cause alarm. He hadn't really expected any signs of Indians. It wasn't at all likely that they were raiding so early in the year, but vigilance could do no harm. Dave wished that Betts shared his opinion. Turning his steps toward the fire, he was greeted with laughter by Betts and the other guards.

"Tell me, Harper," Betts called. "Are the Injuns comin'?"

"There's no sign," Dave said quietly.

"Harper sees Injuns in his sleep," Betts told the others. "He wakes up yellin', 'Don't let 'em sculp me!' You ever see a real live Injun, Harper?"

"I've seen a few," Dave answered. He didn't mind Betts's raillery. The corporal was usually a pleasant man if he wasn't riled, and he was a good soldier, in spite of his ignorance of the frontier. He and the rest of the squad were Hudson Valley farmers, and Dave could understand their lack of concern about Indians. There hadn't been any Indian trouble in their part of the state for almost a hundred years. They had yet to see a seemingly tranquil countryside suddenly burst into flame, to hear the chilling savagery of a Seneca war whoop, to watch hundreds of painted warriors burst from cover with the wild speed of timber wolves. At Stanwix they were comfortable and safe in a strong fortress that the enemy would never dare attack. Here, in this clearing only two miles away, they saw no reason for apprehension.

"The woodcutters are getting hungry," Dave told Betts. "They want to know when we're going to eat."

"Pretty soon," Betts said. "Step in by the fire here and warm yourself, Harper. You make the rest of us feel guilty, standin' out there watchin' for Injuns."

Tim Runnels, tall and skinny and sour-faced, shifted his wad of chewing tobacco and spat a brown stream of juice into the fire. "We ain't got no reason to worry. There ain't an Injun closer than the Genesee. They don't like this weather no more than we do. They stay to home."

"That's right," Betts agreed. "They won't come down

before April, and maybe not then. I think they got a bellyful of this war. All these years of raidin' and burnin', and we're stronger than we ever been."

"They'll come," Dave said. "The weather won't stop them, either."

The corporal laughed. "You can't scare us, Harper. Besides, if they were out, we'd of known it. We got scouts out from the fort all the time. Now you go stir that stew and see if it's ready. We had enough of this here talk about Injuns."

Accompanied by Sam Hawkins, a soldier from the Hudson River town of Kingston who was the only man in the squad his own age, Dave went to the cooking fire and bent over the kettle. The stew didn't smell any better than it usually did. Dave grinned at Sam.

"Hold your nose and it'll taste fine," he said. "My father always said a piece of meat ought to be good and ripe before it's cooked, anyway."

Sam nodded glumly. "Ripe is all right, I guess. This here meat went a little too far, though. That green color kind of turns my stomach, Dave."

"You'll eat worse in your time."

"Maybe so," Sam agreed morosely. "Listen, Dave. You really think the Indians will come down on us?"

"They might not come to Stanwix. They'll go down the valley, though, just the way they do every year. You can bet on it."

"Maybe Betts is right, Dave. Folks say the British would like to quit. More than five years of fighting and they ain't licked us yet. They lost a whole army when Burgoyne surrendered at Saratoga. We got the French on our side now. There's more men in our army than there ever was. They got to quit sometime."

Dave shook his head as he turned his attention once more to the stew. "They're not done yet, Sam. They'll fight us just as long as they got a chance of winning. If Brant and the Rangers make enough big raids this year along the borders, what will Washington feed the army? Grass? That's why they come down on us, Sam. To burn the wheat and the oats and the corn that our folks out here on the frontier send off to the army. That's why we're at Stanwix—to try to keep 'em out of the Mohawk Valley."

"We never see 'em," Sam said. "They go right by and make their raid and then skedaddle. We ought to be back in the middle of the valley, Dave, so we can hit 'em when they come in."

"Don't tell me, Sam," Dave said with a quick grin. "Write a letter to Congress about it."

"I still think the British are ready to quit," Sam said doggedly.

"I think they'll have to make one more big try. Another year, anyway. They've sunk too much into this war. There's another thing, Sam. Remember that the war up here in the Mohawk Valley is different, just as if it had nothing to do with the rest of the fighting. It's just us against Fort Niagara, and they've got more Tory soldiers out there than they've ever had. And the Indians are still boiling mad because Washington sent General Sullivan to burn out the Seneca country year before last. They'll be down, Sam. We'll be seeing 'em."

"I hope I don't see none," Sam said. "That stew ready?"

"I guess it is. Ready as it's ever going to be."

Dave rose from his crouching position, taking his musket from Sam. He was about to wave to the others when his eye caught a flash of motion above the forest west of the clearing. About four hundred yards away, there were five crows circling and swooping against the slate-colored sky. Even against the wind and above the noise the woodcutters were making, he could hear faintly their raucous squalling. He watched them intently. Sam started away, stopped, and looked at Dave puzzledly. He too stared at the western sky and then back at Dave.

"What you lookin' at?" he asked.

"The crows," Dave said. "Something stirred 'em up. They're screaming their heads off."

Sam shrugged. "Crows," he said. "They'll raise a fuss about anything. I'll go tell Betts the stew's ready."

"All right," Dave said, still watching the erratic maneuvering of the birds. Now from the northeast, borne on the sweeping wind, he heard the cries of another flock of crows. He looked that way but couldn't see them. The first flock, in answer to the call of their kind, stopped circling on the western horizon and flew into the wind directly to the northeast. Dave heard them cawing for several seconds after they had vanished across the wall of treetops. Then the sound faded and was gone. He watched and listened, but the forest was quiet again.

Something had disturbed the crows. It might have been the cawing of the flock in the northeast, but if it had been, he should have heard it previously. Perhaps the noise of the woodcutters and the crackling of the fires had drowned out the sound. The incident bothered him. Crows didn't stir about in a high wind.

Betts's voice rose in a cheerful shout. "Hi, you fellers! Come and get it."

The woodcutters left their work in a body, hurrying across the clearing toward the fires. Their tools were dropped carelessly wherever they were working. Their muskets were left stacked on the packed snow of the trail near the sleds.

Betts dipped into the stew with a wooden ladle. "Let the workin' men get theirs first," he said. "There's plenty for everybody." He began to ladle the steaming food into the mess bowls the men held forward.

Dave and Sam stood together, waiting their turn.

"I'd just as lief eat boiled skunk cabbage," Sam said unhappily.

Dave nodded absently. He was still thinking about the crows. He remembered uneasily one of his father's warnings about wilderness campaigning. "If somethin' seems wrong to you, Davey, don't you let it slide. Out in the woods, things should always look natural. If they don't, there's a reason. Find out what it is before you go any farther."

Dave's keen blue eyes were narrowed as he surveyed the perimeter of the forest. There were lines of doubt on his weather-darkened face. He hadn't seen the crows that were calling in the northeast. Suppose there hadn't been any? Indians often used natural forest sounds as signals.

On the ridge northwest of the clearing, a blue jay began to shriek piercingly. Almost instantly another jay answered from the west. Now both of them were scolding excitedly. That wasn't right, either. Their alarm at the arrival of the woodcutting party should have passed long since. The cries they were making were not their usual bad-tempered noise. They were alarmed by some new intruder.

Dave watched the edge of the forest anxiously. The dark barrier of naked trunks and limbs seemed undisturbed. There was something out there that was causing the jays to make a ruckus. Carefully he searched the brush for motion or for a spot of color that was not a part of the drab winter landscape. He couldn't see anything out of the ordinary, but his sense of danger grew stronger and became a certainty. An Indian could hide himself completely in woods as thick as those around the clearing. Dave glanced at the other men, busy with their stew, and made up his mind on the instant. No matter now that Betts would be annoyed. There were Indians out there! Dave knew it. He turned to the corporal.

Then his eye caught a flash of motion on the periphery of the clearing. A fox came out of the brush in a reddish-brown flash of motion. The animal darted over a fallen maple and froze for an instant as it saw the men in the open space; then, veering slightly on its course, crossed the drifts and vanished into the trees on the south side of the clearing. In the few seconds that the animal was in sight, Dave felt relief that he had been wrong about the jays. The fox had scared them. His feeling lasted only until the fox vanished. What had scared the fox?

Dave stepped quickly to Betts's side. "Corporal, you'd better tell the woodcutters to get their muskets. There's trouble coming."

Betts stared at him in amazement. "What kind of trouble, Harper?"

"Indians," Dave said quietly. He nodded toward the western border of the clearing. "I don't know how many. Over there in the woods."

Betts spun around and looked at the dark wall of forest.

His fat red face lost some of its color, and alarm showed in his eyes. Something that might have been fear followed it quickly. He stared at the trees for about five seconds, as if he could see through them. The men were looking wonderingly at him and at Dave. Dave's quiet warning had not been overheard because of the whining of the wind and because most of them had mufflers tied around their ears.

Then the color returned to Betts's face, and it mounted as his anger rose. "Harper, I'm almighty sick and tired of yer foolishness! Injuns, say you! All right, you go look for 'em. Get over there and find 'em. And if you don't, you'll cut wood for the next month."

Dave nodded, flushing as both guards and woodcutters began to laugh at him. "You'd better tell the men to get their muskets, Corporal. I may be right."

He looked to the priming of his weapon and took two steps away from the fire. As if his moving were a signal, a musket cracked in the trees. Its ball plowed into the cooking fire and sent embers flying. The forest seemed to come alive with darting figures. Fierce screams rolled across the clearing. There was a rattle of musketry. The wild yelling seemed to encircle the clearing. The flashes of muskets were everywhere in the trees.

Dave made a leap for the shelter of the nearest felled maple, plunging deep into the snow drifted against it. Other men scattered for cover. Three or four stood where they were, staring stupidly at the forest. Three woodcutters tried to get to their stacked muskets, thirty yards away, but gave up the attempt when bullets furrowed the snow around them and smacked ringingly into the logs and stumps.

Two men burrowed into the snow on either side of Dave. He raised his musket, fired at an orange flash at the edge of the woods, and looked to see who had joined him. On his left was Sam Hawkins, white-faced and shaking. Betts was on his right. The corporal stuck his musket barrel across the log, fired, and began to reload.

"You was right, Harper," Betts said brokenly, without taking his eyes from the trees that hid the enemy. "How many you think they are?"

"I don't know," Dave said. "A lot of 'em. Maybe a hundred."

"There can't be!" Betts cried. "Not that many."

"Lots of muskets shooting at us," Dave said, aiming again. He saw a fur-clad shoulder sticking out from a tree trunk and fired at it. He looked at Betts and had to shout to make himself heard above the musketry and the Indians' wild whooping. "We ought to make a try for those stacked muskets. Just seven of us with guns can't hold 'em off."

Betts looked quickly at his men, all of them now under cover. He shook his head. "It's only two miles to the fort," he said. "They'll hear the shootin' and come after us. We can hold on right here till they come."

The thought of help cheered the corporal. His round red face wrinkled into a savage grin. "Ten minutes and we'll be runnin' those devils right back to Niagara."

Dave watched as Betts aimed his musket. When the corporal had fired with a grunt of satisfaction, Dave touched his arm. He pointed high overhead to the tops of the naked trees, where the wind was whipping the branches. "It's blowing the wrong way," he said. "They won't hear the shooting."

Betts was startled. He stared at the effect of the wind in the trees. The muscles of his jaw tightened as if he were exerting his will to make the wind stop blowing. "You're right," he said finally. "Looks like we're done. I guess you know more than any of us about these Injuns, Harper. What should we do?"

"Go for the muskets," Dave said, "before they jump us. From the sound of that yelling, they're working themselves up to it now."

Betts eyed the thirty yards of open ground that lay between them and the stacked weapons. "All right," he said. "Pass the word along. We'll all run at once and stay there. Plenty of logs and stumps to cover us. Tell 'em to wait for me to yell."

"I'll go around and tell them," Sam Hawkins said. He gave Dave his musket and crawled away, elbow-deep in the snow.

The Indians' fire increased in volume. As if they had guessed the intention to try for the stacked muskets, their bullets whined around any man who moved. Then they began to yell even more fiercely than before. Suddenly two Indians left the cover of the trees, running swiftly but erratically, taking every advantage of the momentary protection of stumps and brush piles. Covered by the heavy fire of their fellows, they were headed for the muskets. Betts rose to his feet and snapped a shot at them. Dave pulled him down. Two other guards stood and fired at the running Indians, but most of the muskets were unloaded. Heavy fire from the trees continued. A man named Morfat pitched forward and lay twisting in the snow, his thigh broken by a musket ball. Tim Runnels dropped his and put his hands to his mouth. Blood streamed over his fingers. Standing in full sight of the enemy, he began to pull broken teeth from his mouth. A musket ball had passed through his cheeks. He stayed there, as if unaware of the bullets that picked at his clothing and whistled around him, until two of the woodcutters pulled his legs from under him.

The two Indians reached the muskets. Without any apparent slowing of their headlong pace, they each wrapped their arms around a stack of the weapons, picked them up, staggered a few feet with them, and then pitched them into a snowbank. They turned instantly and raced back to the shelter of the forest.

Betts stared with despair at the white mound of snow that hid the muskets. "They got us now," he said to Dave. "We ain't got a chance."

Dave thought so too. He couldn't see any way out of the trap. "They'll be coming now," he said. "We'd better get ready."

"We can try to run for the fort," Betts exclaimed. "Every man on his own. They won't catch all of us, and if we stay here we'll all be killed." His voice rose to a shout. "You men! Get ready to run for it."

"No," Dave cried. "They're all around us. Running won't help us."

"What we goin' to do, then?" Betts asked helplessly.

As if in answer to his words, the enemy's fire suddenly stopped. The only sound was the sighing of the wind.

"What's this?" the corporal asked anxiously.

"I don't know," Dave said. "Maybe they're coming."

Then a voice came from the trees, rising above the wind with surprising volume. "You rebels! Listen to me."

There was a pause, and then the voice called: "Do you hear me?"

Whoever it was, Dave Harper had heard him before. It was a resonant, commanding voice, charged with authority and confidence. The tone was that of an educated man. Again the call came: "Do you hear me, rebels?"

Betts cautiously poked his head above the log. "We hear you. Who are you? What you got to say?"

In the second or two before the man called once more, Dave Harper wrung his memory for the identity of that voice. It had been years ago that he had heard it—before the war, surely, and in peaceful conversation. It had been a pleasant voice then, friendly and humorous, and it had said—— What were the words? The scene came back to Dave: the road in front of the Harper cabin in Cherry Valley, and his father talking of the old days of the French War, talking to a tall, broad man with a bronze-colored face who was elegantly dressed in the clothing of the gentry. His father had said, pointing to the slender boy who stared at the handsome stranger: "This is Davey, Joseph. He is my oldest."

The stranger had made a playful motion to cuff the boy on the shoulder, had laughed, and then the deep ringing voice had said: "Will you make a woodsrunner of him, Nat?"

Dave knew who it was.

"Rebels, listen to me! My men are all around you. You cannot escape. Put down your weapons and come out. We will not harm you. I give you my word."

"We can't," Betts whispered. "We can't. They'll kill us, anyways." He was shaking and shivering. He looked once

in the direction of the fort, as if expecting to see a line
of blue-clad Continentals come running along the trail.

"I will give you one minute to decide," the man in the
forest shouted. "Surrender or be killed."

Dave gripped Betts's arm. "I know him," he said. "It's
Joseph Brant."

"Brant!" Betts exclaimed. "Then we're as good as dead.
Brant's the worst of them all." He hunched closer to the
shelter of the log, as if more protection were necessary
now that he knew who the enemy was. While most of the
soldiers in the garrisons of the Mohawk Valley had never
seen Joseph Brant, his reputation as the leader of the Six
Nations was known to them all. Countless tales of savagery along the border had transformed Brant in the
minds of both regulars and militiamen into a legendary
figure so powerful and invincible that it was useless to op-
pose him.

Corporal Betts was frightened for the first time in more
than five years of war. He had faced British regulars on
Long Island, Hessians at Saratoga, and Tory troops in
New Jersey, and had never lost the courage that was part
of his plodding, stubborn nature. But he had never seen a
hostile Indian, and the picture of a screaming line of
painted savages bursting from the forest unnerved him.
Dave Harper watched Betts anxiously as the corporal
huddled by the log, biting his lips.

"I know Brant's voice," Dave urged. "That's who it is.
We'd better do what he says, Corporal."

As if Dave's words had been a dash of cold water, Betts
started, shook himself nervously, and then regained his
control.

"What do you mean, Harper?"

"We'd better give up."

"No! They'll kill us all. We'll fight. We got to fight." He shoved his musket over the edge of the log and stared at the forest. "Fight! That's the only thing," he whispered.

"We can't fight," Dave said quietly. "They'd wipe us out in the first rush. We can't run. We can only surrender."

"Better to fight than get killed," Betts answered.

"My father used to tell me that Joseph Brant is a man of his word," Dave said firmly. He didn't really believe that himself, but it was their only chance. In spite of what his father had said in praise of Brant in the days before the war, Dave remembered it was Brant who was blamed for loosing the Indians at Cherry Valley. Nevertheless, he repeated Brant's promise to Betts. "He says they won't hurt us."

"Maybe," Betts said dubiously. He lifted himself sufficiently to look around at the other men, grouped in twos and threes behind logs and stumps. They were all watching him anxiously, waiting for a decision. The only sounds were the harsh whining of the wind in the trees and the weakening cries of pain from Morfat, who had crawled to the cover of a log and now lay there dully watching the blood pump from his wound. Betts turned his eyes back to Dave. "You seem to know Injuns, Harper. You're the only one who does. You really think he means it?"

"We'll have to take his word," Dave said sharply. The people at Cherry Valley, he remembered, had knelt in the snow to beg for mercy, but they'd been cut down ruthlessly.

Brant called from the forest: "Time is up, rebels. Will you surrender?"

Betts gripped his musket tightly. Then he nodded his head. "Tell him yes," he whispered to Dave.

Dave rose to his feet slowly, tensing himself against the chance that a volley of musket balls would smash him down. There was no sound or movement in the forest, although he knew that a hundred musket barrels were lined on his chest. He dropped his musket. "We give up," he shouted.

"All of you stand up," Brant answered. "Leave your weapons on the ground."

Slowly the woodcutters and the guards rose from their shelters. Still not an enemy showed himself. Then, like partridges bursting from dense cover, a wave of Indians came out of the trees. They fanned into the shape of a scimitar that swept upon the prisoners and then closed around them. Behind the Indians were about thirty white men in green uniform jackets and buckskin leggings.

Brant came with the white men, striding a few paces before them. He was accompanied by an officer in a green jacket.

As the Indians approached, the prisoners moved together into a compact group. They waited tensely for the first sign of the violence that most of them expected. It didn't come. The Indians scattered to pick up muskets, axes, and saws. They dug into the snow to pull out the muskets that had been thrown there. Several of them hefted the sledge hammers the woodcutters used to split logs. They obviously thought the sixteen-pound weights far too heavy to carry as plunder, because they dropped them into the snow.

Brant stood in the trail about twenty yards from the prisoners, seemingly paying no attention to them. He watched his men. A pair of Indians bent over the cooking fire. One of them dipped out a ladleful of stew, smelled it, and grimaced. The other Indian laughed, then the pair of them kicked the legs of the tripod until the kettle fell into the fire. A half dozen Indians gathered around the two yoke of oxen. They seemed to be arguing. Apparently some of them wanted to take the oxen and sleds with them. A sharp command from Brant to one of the green-coated soldiers ended the matter. The soldier, with a dour look as if he didn't like the task, picked up one of the abandoned sledge hammers, walked up to the second yoke of oxen, and swung the sledge above his head. He killed the nigh ox with one blow. Before the animal had slumped in the great wooden yoke, the off ox was struck in the head. Then the soldier stepped to the heads of the lead pair, killed them both, and flipped the sledge into the snow, where it sank from sight.

Jeptha Wilson, standing beside Dave Harper, spat into the snow. The oxen had been his charges. Dave turned anxiously to him. This would be a bad time for Wilson to start trouble, but there was no reason to worry. A faint grin twisted Wilson's face as his eyes met Dave's. "They should of loosed them cattle from the yokes before they killed 'em," Wilson said. "Ever try to get a yoke off a dead ox?"

The Indians, several dozen of them, weren't troubled by the oxbows. They went to work on the oxen where they lay, hacking them to pieces with tomahawks and knives.

"Them beasts will be tough eatin'," Wilson said softly.

Brant finally seemed to take notice of the prisoners. He and the green-coated officer came forward. "Who's in command here?" Brant asked in his deep voice.

"I am," Betts answered.

"What's your rank?"

"Corporal."

"Line your men up for inspection, Corporal. Two files, and have them stand at attention."

There was a momentary interruption. Morfat, lying on the ground nearby, cried out as the pain in his wounded leg suddenly became more severe. Brant turned and looked at him. Morfat screamed again. The Indian leader walked over and bent down to look at the wound. Morfat had fainted. Brant lifted the man's hand and tested his pulse, then looked again at the wound and at the stream of bright arterial blood that pumped from it. He got up, spoke briefly to a nearby Indian, and walked away. The Indian ran up to Morfat, drawing his tomahawk from his belt. Most of the prisoners turned their eyes away. Sam Hawkins cried out in terror, putting his hands over his face.

Dave saw the tomahawk rise and fall. He knew why Brant had ordered it—Morfat was dying. Nothing could have been done for him, but the swift brutality was sickening. Dave looked at the green-coated soldiers. They showed no signs of emotion at Morfat's death. Their faces were grim and hard-bitten; their eyes viewed the prisoners with sharp hostility, and two of them were laughing harshly at some quiet joke. They were Butler's Rangers, who had served so long with the Indians that the sudden outburst of savagery had little effect upon them. The people of Cherry Valley, Dave knew, would say that these Tory renegades were capable of deeds far worse than any invented by the Indians. Dave wondered how many of these thirty were from the Mohawk Valley settlements, for he knew that John Butler had recruited most of his corps from loyalists who had fled to Canada from the frontier villages of New York and Pennsylvania. He wondered bitterly if one of them had fired the shot that had killed his father at Cherry Valley.

Brant faced the prisoners again. To Dave he seemed unconcerned and in no hurry to get away as he looked at each of the prisoners in turn. They stared back. Tim Runnels was muttering angrily through bloody lips. Dave had his first opportunity to observe Brant closely.

The Indian was not the giant that he had seemed to be years before in Cherry Valley. He had broad shoulders and a thick chest, and there were obvious power and grace in his heavy frame. However, he was physically no bigger than many of the soldiers who faced him. It was his face, Dave decided, that fostered the impression of size and strength and had given rise to the legends along the New York frontier that Brant was the tallest, strongest, and most ferocious of his people. His face was broad and heavy-boned, and the flesh was lumped as if it had been battered and beaten into its present shape. Across his broad brow and on his cheeks were a few scattered pits left by smallpox. His complexion seemed darker than it had years ago, but Dave imagined that was the effect of weathering by wind and sun. His eyes were dark, seeming almost black as Brant slitted them against the glare of the snow.

When he spoke, his voice was deep and measured, as if he chose the words carefully because of pride in his cultured speech. "I am Joseph Brant," he said. "You have heard of me?"

Several of the prisoners nodded quickly.

"You will not be harmed," Brant said, "unless you try to escape, or make trouble, or fail to keep the pace we set. If you do any of these things, my Mohawks will kill you. It is a long way back to Niagara, through rough country, and with snow lying deep in the woods. Once we have started, we will stop only for meals and sleeping. Make up your minds that you must keep going, because if you fall behind, there will be only one warning. There is no objection to any of you helping those who may need help, but don't fall behind! Do any of you have any questions?"

Betts started to speak and then thought better of it.

"What is it, Corporal?" Brant asked.

"Him," Betts said, pointing to Morfat's body. "If you don't mean us no harm, how come you killed him?"

Brant nodded gravely. "I have come to be something of a physician. The man was dying. He might have lived another hour. I ended his suffering."

The Indian leader spoke a few words in the harsh Mohawk language to one of the Indians nearby, who reached into his hunting bag and brought out a hidebound order book and a lead stylus. Brant took them and turned again to the prisoners.

"Each of you will give me your name and rank," he said. "Some of you may not reach Niagara, and this record must be kept for the exchange of prisoners after the war."

He moved along the line of captives, writing each man's name in his book. When he reached Tim Runnels standing next to Dave, he inspected Runnels' torn face with interest. "You must have had your mouth wide open," Brant said. "You are lucky, my friend. That ball should have broken your jaw. As it is, you won't be able to chew meat for a while, but you'll be all right."

Brant turned to Dave. "Name and rank," he said.

"David Harper, private soldier."

The name caught Brant's attention. He looked searchingly at Dave. "Where are you from, Harper?"

"Cherry Valley, before you burned it," Dave said harshly.

Brant looked steadily at him. "Nathan Harper was your father?"

"That's right."

Brant nodded gravely. "I see his face in yours. He and I were old friends. We used to hunt together in the old days. We fought side by side in the French War. You know that your father was my friend?"

"You and your men killed him at Cherry Valley!"

Brant's face darkened with quick anger, but it faded almost as quickly as it came. "I would have done anything I could to save him, young Harper, but I could not have been everywhere in the valley that day. Nor could Walter Butler. I found your father's body in the snow. I am sorry. His memory will always be in my heart."

Dave didn't answer. His eyes met Brant's with a cold stare. The Indian finally nodded in his grave manner and wrote Dave's name in his order book. Then he moved along the line.

When the roll of prisoners was completed, Brant gave orders for the swift packing of the meat from the butchered oxen and the bundling of the woodcutters' tools. These burdens were distributed among the prisoners. Then the column was formed. The Indians were in the lead, the captives were in the center, and the green-coated, hard-faced soldiers of Butler's Rangers brought up the rear. A long powerful call from Brant brought four Mohawks from the forest in the direction of the fort where they had been watching for the first sign of a sortie by the garrison. The captives supposed that their absence would not be noted now until somebody in the fort wondered what had happened to the woodcutting party.

The route was west by southwest toward Oneida Lake. The raw wind seemed colder and more penetrating, and as the column vanished into the shadows of the timbered hills the gray sky kept its promise of snow. Driven by the wind, the snow billowed and swirled in the clearing, drifting high against the loaded sleds, covering the remains of the oxen, and forming a white mound to mark the spot where Morfat's body lay.

CHAPTER TWO

The Indians and Rangers had snowshoes; the prisoners had none. For the first few hours the traveling was not difficult, because the Indians at the head of the column packed the base snow into a firm path for those who followed. By midafternoon, however, as the snowfall continued, the captives were plowing through knee-high drifts, dragging their legs and stumbling as exhaustion gripped them.

The snow cut into their faces. Whipped by the icy wind, it stung and bit their flesh. They walked with heads down to breathe without drawing the bitter air into their lungs. Their arms and legs were numb with cold.

When a man slipped or stumbled and fell, his companions stared at him for a second or two in dull wonder, as if amazed that he should be so stupid as to let himself go down. Then clumsily they set him on his feet again and pushed him forward, supporting him as well as they could for a few yards until he picked up the shuffling rhythm of the step again.

Brant evidently feared pursuit, once the fort discovered the fate of the woodcutters, even though the tracks of the party were quickly covered by the shifting snow. He posted a dozen Indians to watch the back trail. This was Oneida country, and the Oneidas were the only nation of the Iroquois Confederacy active in the American cause. If Oneida scouts led a rescue party from Fort Stanwix, they'd find the raiders even in the storm, and Brant knew how easily his force could be scattered and cut down in a running fight through a storm.

Brant ranged the length of the column during the march, his powerful figure wrapped in a blue cloak against the fury of the wind-driven snow. His deep voice occasionally rolled over the noise of the elements as he issued commands to his Indians. Sometimes he marched beside the Ranger captain, sometimes alone, and often he faded back into the dark forest to take the reports of the flankers and the rear guard. He paid little attention to the prisoners until, toward the end of the afternoon, he fell into step beside Dave Harper. Dave looked up from the endless, exhausting monotony of pulling one foot after the other through the snow. He saw Brant's hard dark eyes fixed on his face.

"Can you keep going, young Harper?" Brant said suddenly.

"I can make it," Dave said grimly.

"And the rest of them?" Brant said, gesturing with a slight wave of his hand at the hunched, stumbling figures of the Continentals. "We cannot let any of them fall behind."

"We'll carry them if we have to," Dave said.

Brant studied him for a minute without replying. Then he smiled swiftly and spoke in curiously mild tones. "You're the picture of your father. You even talk like him. You sound as if you've had some schooling."

"My mother kept school for us every day," Dave answered shortly.

"Where is she now?" Brant asked.

"In Schoharie," Dave said. "At my uncle's farm."

"Believe me," Brant said quietly. "I am sorry about your father. He and I ran the woods together when we were boys. He stayed in my father's house at Canajoharie. I taught him the Mohawk and Seneca languages. When the French War came, we fought side by side. Did he ever tell you about those days?"

"He used to speak of you often," Dave admitted unwillingly. "That was before the war. He changed his mind about you when you went to Canada."

"Yes," the Indian said. "He thought I should have been a rebel and should have taken my Mohawks into your army. Is that right?"

Dave hesitated. He remembered his father's bitterness toward Joseph Brant, who had led more raids against the frontier than any of the enemy leaders at Niagara, whose name alone was enough to make women shudder and children cry. Dave answered reluctantly. "My father said you had changed. He said that the man who used to be his friend would not lead Indians against women and children."

"They are my people," Brant answered harshly. "They fight for the King in their way as you fight against him in yours. We did not start the war, young Harper." He paused briefly. "Did you know Sir William Johnson?"

"I saw him a few times," Dave said. "My father knew him."

"He was a great man," Brant said simply. "There has never been a white man who understood and loved my people more than Sir William, and I think there will never be another. He was a second father to me, young Harper. He took me into his house, educated me, taught me the Christian religion. He married my sister Molly. He was as American as you are, although he was born in Ireland. He loved this country very deeply and he taught me to love it in the same way. But above all, young Harper, he was loyal to the King who gave him his honors. Sir William was the King's Indian agent for North America. He was the one white man my people knew they could trust without fear. All I have I owe to Sir William Johnson, including my loyalty to King George. I never for a moment thought of giving my services and those of my Mohawks to your rebel Congress."

"Sir William died before the war," Dave said stubbornly. "How do you know he wouldn't have declared for Congress?"

"I knew his heart and mind as well as I know my own," Brant answered. "He was a King's man always, and so am I."

As suddenly as he had come, Brant vanished into the storm and the gathering darkness. Dave tucked his chin into the folds of his coat and fastened his eyes again on the heels of the man in front of him as the column sloughed its way inexorably westward toward the limits of the Oneida country, where the danger of pursuit would end.

Brant's words lingered in Dave's mind. He admitted to himself that Sir William would probably have declared for the King if he had lived to see the war come. Probably it was fortunate for the rebellion that Sir William was not leading the King's forces in New York. He had been a man of power and brilliance, and as leader of the Indians and Tories he would have hammered at the frontier with mighty blows. The whole course of the war might have been changed, Dave supposed, if Sir William Johnson had lived to direct the border war. Brant and the Butlers were effective leaders, but they lacked the power to command and achieve that Johnson had carried to his grave.

Corporal Betts stumbled forward from somewhere in the rear and fell into step beside Dave. "I seen you talkin' to him, Harper. What did he say they was goin' to do with us?"

"We didn't talk about that."

"Every time one of us goes down, them Rangers look mean. You think they'd kill us if we couldn't keep goin'? Some of the men is near beat."

Dave kept his head down to hide a quick smile. Until this morning he'd been, in Betts's eyes, just another young soldier among many, a fellow who annoyed veterans of five years of war with wild tales about Indians. Now his position was changed. His father had been Brant's friend; Dave was a trained woodsman; he knew something about Indians. The veteran had come to the recruit for advice and encouragement.

"I think we're ready to stop," Dave said. "They won't try to keep going in the storm after it gets dark. The going will be easier from now on. Tomorrow we'll be in their country."

"How far you think it is to Niagara?" Betts asked. "I seen it on maps at Stanwix. Looks like a long way."

"About a hundred and eighty miles."

"That will take eight days, the way they're movin'. I don't know if we can keep up without snowshoes."

Dave knew that it would be nearer four days, depending on the storm. He remembered his father's story of the Mohawk runner in the French War who had covered the three hundred miles between Niagara and Fort Johnson in less than five days. Betts was used to marching with an army that considered fifteen or twenty miles a good day's travel. But Dave kept his opinion to himself; Betts had enough to worry about.

The corporal's next words showed that he was worrying. "You get a chance, Harper," he said, "you talk again to Brant. Find out what's goin' to happen to us. The men are pretty scared. They're all talkin' about runnin' the gantlet. They've heard about it. They say only a few gets through it alive."

Dave tried to reassure him. "If we go straight through to Niagara, we won't have to worry about that. The British wouldn't let the Indians do it."

"Who says they won't? And suppose we don't go to Niagara? Suppose we stop in one of the Injun towns. They'll do what they want with us then, won't they?"

Dave said he didn't think so. Into his mind came a picture of two parallel lines of raging Indians, armed with clubs and spears, waiting with savage anticipation for the prisoners to try to stumble through the storm of blows. He supposed that if the British didn't intervene, the ordeal of the gantlet might lay ahead of the captives.

Betts had another thought. "What about these Rangers? I don't trust 'em. Looks to me like they'd just as soon kill a man as look at him."

Dave shook his head. "I don't think they're as black as they're painted," he said. "They were accused of things at Cherry Valley that they had no part in. They may have killed my father—more likely them than the Indians—but he was carrying a rifle and trying to get to the fort. They look hard enough, but they wouldn't kill prisoners just for the fun of it. You can see for yourself that they're well disciplined. They'll do what their officers say."

"Maybe you're right," Betts said. "But can we trust their officers? Anyway, you keep your ears open. Maybe you'll hear something from Brant."

"I'll let you know if I do," Dave answered.

Brant called a halt soon afterward in desolate wooded country, a long shallow valley between two ridges. Even the company of Butler's Rangers, woodsmen who were used to bedding down wherever they found themselves at nightfall, looked around them with sour faces when the order came to halt. They didn't relish the idea of scraping a campsite in the tangle of laurel and stunted evergreens that poked above the drifted snow. The prisoners didn't care where they camped. They were exhausted. Some of them sat in the snow and went to sleep with their heads on their folded arms.

At Brant's command two Indians clambered up the slope on the left, vanishing in the darkness. The column waited. Three or four minutes later there was a faint hail from the slope. Brant shouted a command, and the party began to climb the slope, following the trail left by the two Indians. Some of the prisoners had to be dragged by their companions.

Halfway up the slope the climbers found a series of cave-like indentations in the face of the ridge. The snow had not drifted heavily into the recesses. They were sheltered from the wind by the overhang of rock, and there was room enough for the entire party to get out of the storm.

"A shelter place," Dave said to Betts. "They must have used it before. Brant knew right where it was."

There was no reason now to prohibit campfires. The prisoners who had some strength left were put to bringing in the limbs of storm-felled trees on the slope, while a fierce-looking Seneca passed along the ledges doling out coals from the fire keeper he had carried all day long through the storm. The fire keeper was a section of hickory log, hollowed by fire, filled with glowing coals from the last campsite, and capped at the open end with a piece of rawhide. Small holes bored into the wood permitted just enough air to circulate inside to keep the coals glowing.

The prisoners were assigned a ledge between the Rangers and the several dozen Senecas who were their guards. They were all hungry after the long day without food, but the Senecas paid no attention to them when food was being prepared. After the Indians had eaten, however, the captives were given great chunks of the stringy ox meat to sear over the coals of their fires. The Indian who had given them the meat also provided a leather sack full of powdered corn mixed with maple sugar. There was enough in the sack to furnish each prisoner with a handful. Otherwise neither Indians nor Rangers gave any sign that the Continental soldiers were under surveillance. It was a quiet camp. Most of the raiding party rolled themselves in their blankets and went to sleep.

The prisoners ate ravenously. Even Tim Runnels managed to swallow balls of fat dipped into the corn meal. After they had all eaten, they made the best sleeping arrangements possible. Wrapped in their coats, they lay as near to the fires as they could get without burning themselves. None of them had blankets, so they huddled together on the cold stone floor of the ledge, trying to share the heat of their bodies.

The Ranger captain, a grim-faced young man named Andrew Bradt, left his men and came to inspect the prisoners. It was the first time he or any of his men had given more than passing attention to the captives. Dave had noticed that the Rangers always kept to themselves, on the march as well as here in camp, although all of them seemed to be at ease with their Indian allies.

"It's going to be a cold night," Bradt said abruptly to Betts. "Your men will freeze. They can't march with frozen feet." His gaze took in the men who were still awake: Dave, Sam Hawkins, and Tim Runnels. "You four go down the slope and get wood for your fires. You'll have to get enough to keep 'em goin' all night."

"Thanks," Betts said in surprise.

"Keep your thanks, rebel," the captain said coldly. "Rebels and traitors are more valuable as prisoners than as dead men. Step along now! My men will give you axes."

Under a guard of two Rangers, the four prisoners left the ledges and walked down the slope to a tangled mass of trees brought down by a storm in years gone by. A large working party of Rangers was cutting wood for their own fires. Some of the Indians were also working at dead trees farther along the slope.

The snow had stopped a half hour before, and in the eastern sky there was a faint glow of moonlight behind the scudding clouds. It became steadily clearer, and soon its radiance on the snow gave them plenty of light for working. Betts and Dave did the chopping, Sam Hawkins trimmed the logs, and Runnels gathered them for the long carry up the slope. They worked on several pines that lay together in the tangled mass of brush, while the Rangers were cutting logs from a similar blow-down about thirty yards away.

While he worked, Dave thought unhappily of the warmth and comfort of Fort Stanwix and the casual pleasures of garrison life there. He'd expected fighting when he'd joined the Continental line. When he was with the militia, they'd chased raiders up and down the Mohawk Valley, but they hadn't done any real fighting. He'd joined the regular army to do his share in driving the Indians and Tories from the frontier, but he'd been disappointed when the Stanwix garrison had remained inactive. There had been no fighting in his months at the fort. Raiders gave Stanwix a wide berth because it was too strong to be attacked and taken. The enemy well remembered the fiasco of the St. Leger expedition in 1777. St. Leger had brought almost a thousand men, Indians and loyalists, to Stanwix with the intention of taking the fort and marching through the Mohawk Valley to Albany, where he was supposed to join Burgoyne's army. St. Leger had been stopped at Oriskany, a few miles from Stanwix, by the Mohawk Valley militia under General Herkimer.

Dave had anticipated fighting when he came to Stanwix, but instead had found only guard duty and drill. He had fretted at the inactivity sometimes, thinking he'd be of more use in winning the war if he'd stayed with his mother and brothers on his uncle's farm in Schoharie where at least he would have been kept busy growing the grain needed so badly by the army. Now, he thought ruefully, how gladly he'd exchange his present lot for life at the fort.

Dave had many friends at Stanwix. One in particular meant a great deal to him—Hannah Armstrong, the daughter of a widow who had a post as trader and merchant for the garrison and the civilian families. He remembered the first time he had seen Hannah when he had visited her mother's store to buy an extra pair of wool socks. She had been standing behind the plank counter, bright-eyed and vivacious, laughing at the horseplay of a half dozen soldiers who were supposed to be customers but were obviously more interested in Hannah than in the store's merchandise. She had dark red hair that hung loosely down to her shoulders. When she moved quickly or threw back her head to laugh, the red hair reflected bronze flashes of sunlight. She had a sprinkling of freckles across her nose. Her eyes were blue. Dave thought she was the prettiest girl he had ever seen and he stood dumbly near the counter that first day, watching her joke with the soldiers. He forgot his reason for being there until a quiet, amused voice spoke at his elbow.

"Can I help you, young man, or will you wait for Hannah?"

He looked vaguely at the pleasant gray-haired woman who had spoken to him, and then stared again at the girl. "Is that her name?" he asked absently.

"Hannah Armstrong," the woman said. "I am her mother. What is it you want?"

Dave bought his stockings and left the store, wildly envious of the soldiers who were lucky enough to talk to Hannah. After that he managed to visit the store at least once a day, and sometimes more often, budgeting his meager pay to buy tobacco that he didn't use, rock candy that he gave to his messmates, needles, pins, buttons, shoe buckles, hatbands, and other gimcracks, until he had enough stock, he thought ruefully, to start a store of his own.

It seemed ages to Dave before Hannah was greeting him with the same warm friendliness that she showed to other men in the regiment, and Dave fully expected a refusal the first time he asked her to go with him to Sunday-morning church services.

She accepted, however, and he was proud as she walked beside him across the parade ground to the church. He knew that the eyes of every young man in the regiment were following him with envy. She asked him to dinner following the services, and soon it became the custom for Dave to take her to church when he was off duty and to have dinner afterward with her and her mother. He considered himself lucky to be so favored, but he couldn't understand it, when there were so many soldiers who knew more of the ways of women than he did.

He didn't know that Hannah had noticed him immediately the first time he came into the store, and had later asked her mother about the young man with the dark hair and sun-tanned face. Nor did Sam Hawkins tell Dave that Hannah had plagued him for the full life history of the new soldier from Cherry Valley.

Stanwix was a dull post to most of the men in the garrison. But for Dave Harper, the months passed swiftly and happily. Before the winter was over, he knew that he would, whenever he could summon the courage, ask Hannah Armstrong to go home with him to Cherry Valley as his wife. But there had never seemed to be an appropriate time, and he had not yet asked her.

His friendship with Hannah had done much to ease the bitterness that the war had brought him—the death of his father, the loss of their home at Cherry Valley, and the long separation from his mother and the boys. It was enough that the future seemed to hold bright prospects.

Now as he thought about that future he was troubled. He'd probably never get the opportunity to ask Hannah to marry him. There was nothing ahead but bleak days. He might not survive the arduous march to Niagara. He couldn't believe in Brant's word as a guarantee of safety. The Indians might make him run the gantlet, and even if he lived through that ordeal he might be a captive for years. There was no reason to assure himself that Hannah would welcome him when he returned at the end of the war; during his captivity she might marry any one of a hundred suitors among the Stanwix garrison. After all, she was bound by no promise to Dave.

With the memory of Hannah on his mind as he swung his ax into the yielding pine logs, Dave thought hopelessly of the prospects of escaping once the war party reached Niagara. It would be almost impossible, he knew, to cut and run from a strong British fort situated in the heart of the Indian country. He wouldn't have a chance, even with his knowledge of the big woods, to elude the Indians who would be sent after him. It was likely that the prisoners from Stanwix would be kept at Niagara; they were the property of the Mohawks and Senecas under Brant, and, as any man who served on the frontier knew, the Indians disliked turning their captives over to the British for exchange.

Logically, therefore, Dave's thoughts swung to the idea of attempting escape even before the war party reached Niagara, and he made up his mind to take the first chance that came along.

The two guards were huddled against a rock outcropping halfway between the two working parties of Rangers and prisoners. The wind was piercingly cold, and the guards were more concerned about escaping its bitter blasts than in watching the prisoners.

Dave glanced at them frequently as he swung his double-bitted ax in unison with Betts's rhythmic chopping. When he and the corporal had worked well into the mass of dead limbs, Dave managed a whispered conversation.

"They're not keeping a close eye on us," he said. "I could make a run for it, and I think I could make it. One of us ought to get back with word of what happened. Maybe the colonel sent a party out after us. If I found 'em, I could lead 'em back."

Betts stopped chopping, and he looked at Dave in amazement. "Don't be a fool, Harper! They'd get you before you made a hundred yards. Like as not they'd kill you."

"Keep working," Dave whispered. "And don't raise your voice."

"You'd be crazy to try it," Betts said anxiously. "You ain't got snowshoes, nor weapons. They'd get you sure."

"I've been in the woods before," Dave said quietly. "All I need is a start. I'll be all right if I can get a few miles ahead of them. Here's what I'll do. We'll carry the wood up to the fires, because if I pulled foot before that, they wouldn't let you keep bringing wood. On the last trip I'll slide into these bushes, crawl down into the valley, and then get up and run."

"They'll see you go! They'll put the Injuns after you."

"I'll pick a time when they're not looking this way. Notice how they keep their faces down inside their collars."

"There's somethin' you ain't thought of, Harper. What happens to us if you get away? It'll go hard with us. You ought to think about that."

"They won't blame you for something I do. The worst that can happen is that they'll watch you closer."

"I don't like it," Betts growled. "You're sure to get killed, Harper. That won't rest easy with me." He paused, looking uneasily at Dave.

"Keep working!" Dave urged.

Betts resumed his powerful swings, spacing his words between the ringing blows of the ax. "I can't let you do it. It's too risky for you and may mean trouble for the rest of us."

"You can't stop me," Dave said grimly. "The only thing you can do is tell them I'm going to run."

"You know I wouldn't do that," Betts said hastily.

"All right, then," Dave said. "Let's get the wood cut. The sooner we get finished, the sooner I start for Stanwix."

It was exhausting labor to haul the heavy sections of pine up the hill, even though they used ropes furnished by the Rangers to pull the wood over the snow. Betts awakened four of the sleeping prisoners and ordered them to help. Tim Runnels had to quit working; his jaw throbbed with pain every time he heaved on the rope. The rest of the camp had settled down by the time the prisoners were ready to haul the last load. The two Ranger guards called peevishly for more speed; they too wanted the warmth of the fires.

Seven men stumbled wearily down the hill and into the brush for the last of the firewood. Six of them returned, their backs bowed against the strain of the ropes. Dave Harper crouched in the brush, knowing how senseless it would be to dash away in the bright moonlight if the guards noticed that one man was missing. They didn't, however. They followed the prisoners up the hill, their heads still lowered and their shoulders hunched against the wind. Dave grinned exultantly when the prisoners vanished behind the glare of the fires. The two Rangers joined their sleeping fellows. Here and there on the ledges close to the prisoners Dave could see the silhouettes of several Indian sentries. He hoped he was deep enough in the brush to escape their notice.

He crawled away through the snow, staying on his hands and knees until he reached the trail in the valley below. The fires now were only spots of orange light flickering through the trees. The trail, packed firmly by the passage of almost two hundred men during the storm, had gathered another inch or so of light snow, not enough to blot it out or to hinder his stride.

He turned eastward on the trail and began to run. His muscles were sore from the long forced march of the day and from the labor of woodcutting. His body cried for rest. He was smiling, however, as he felt the reserves of strength flow into his long legs. He settled into an easy stride that under normal conditions he could have maintained for the better part of a day without resting. Since boyhood he had followed game trails and trap lines with his father and had worked on the Harper farm from sunup until sunset. He was strong and lithe and knew that if he had a full night's start on his pursuers the best runners among the Indians couldn't catch him before he reached Stanwix. He would have to stop and rest sometime, but so would the Indians who would pursue him. They had traveled as far the day before as he had.

The moon cast a brilliant light on the snow. Dave could see the trail clearly for a hundred yards ahead of him. Sometimes he had to slow down and pick his way when a cloud crossed the face of the moon. The wind was dying rapidly, and the cold air no longer hurt his mouth and throat. His lungs adjusted to the demands of his pace after the first half mile, and he moved steadily and silently through the dark forest, a fleeting shadow against the white background of the snow.

CHAPTER THREE

The weather began to change with dawn. The wind was blowing again, but now it came out of the southeast. It was a different wind from the bitter one of the day before. This was a seasonal March blow that brought warm air rolling up from the south. In its first hour it had no effect on the dry snow underfoot, which began to pack instead of swirl as Dave pulled his weary legs through it. The temperature was rising. As soon as the sun came up, the snow would begin melting.

Dave had almost reached the limit of his endurance. His legs were sore and heavy and his lungs sucked air in short, painful gasps. He knew he would have to rest. He had no idea how far he had run, because this country was new to him and he recognized no landmarks. He knew that Stanwix couldn't be too far away, however; he had been running all night at a greater speed than the war party had made going west the day before.

He thought he was safe. They had probably just discovered his absence and started in pursuit. They had many more miles to cover before they reached this place than he had ahead of him to Stanwix. He had time to rest.

He picked his sleeping place with care. It was a small

cutbank of gravel and shale beside a frozen brook. He scraped the snow clear at the base of the cutbank and lay down directly underneath the overhanging lip. Drifted snow was perched on the lip like a breaking wave. As soon as the sun and the wind brought the temperature up, that snow would fall and wake him. From the feel of the weather, he thought he'd have about three hours sleep before the snow melted.

He lay on the cold bed of shale and was almost instantly asleep, in spite of the gradual chill that crept through his body.

As he had expected, the first bits of snow fell from the lip of the cutbank when the sun was about three hours high in the sky. The snow fell lightly on his body, but he didn't awaken. Then a large chunk shivered, moved an inch or so, hung on the edge of the bank for another minute, and fell heavily on his chest. He awoke with a start.

Every muscle in his body complained when he pushed himself to his feet. He was shaking with cold. He flexed his arms and legs. Then he moved stiffly to the edge of the brook and kicked a hole in the ice with his boot. He drank deeply. The water was so cold it made his teeth ache. Painfully he moved back to the trail. He decided to walk a half mile, steadily increasing his speed as his muscles loosened, before he tried to run again.

The brook lay in a shallow cut in the rolling land. He walked slowly to the top of the rise above it, pumping his arms to get the blood circulating. He paused on the rise, looking ahead, hoping that perhaps he could see Fort Stanwix in the far distance, but he didn't really expect to see it; he couldn't be that close. There was nothing in sight but great stretches of dark forest, patched here and there by dazzling white spots of snow in the blow-downs.

He turned and looked at his back trail. It was the same, nothing but mile after mile of trees and snow. High in the sky above the forest a hawk soared effortlessly. It was the only moving thing Dave saw. Then his heart jumped and a soft cry caught in his throat. Something had moved back there—something that he knew immediately was a man, although he had seen only a blur of motion. He shaded his eyes against the glare of the sun reflecting from the snow, watching a small natural clearing more than a mile away. The trail crossed the center of the clearing. He could see, even at this distance, the faint grayish patch cutting across the whiteness where hundreds of feet had tamped the snow the day before.

As he watched, four men ran across the clearing in single file. They were coming swiftly; for a couple of seconds they were in view, and then they were gone.

Dave turned and started to run. Every part of his body protested, but he tucked his arms close to his sides, pumping them easily in rhythm with his stride as he picked it up. His long legs faltered, stumbled, and then stretched out. He tried to breathe evenly and slowly in spite of the pain in his chest and lungs.

He realized now that he should have kept going instead of taking time to sleep. Stanwix couldn't be three hours away; he'd probably already be there if he hadn't slept. He'd hoped for more time. They must have discovered that he was missing last night soon after he'd left. He knew he couldn't keep the pace he was setting himself. A mile or two and he'd be winded. He would be forced to slow down; he would stumble and fall. He knew that his pursuers must be tired, too, but they must have been picked because of their endurance. It was too much to hope that he could outrun four of them.

He held his speed doggedly. His chest burned as if it were afire, and his legs were leaden. All the strength seemed gone from them. With fumbling fingers he unbuttoned his coat and dropped it in the trail. The loss of its weight seemed to add to his speed for a minute or two, but then he began to feel exhaustion again. He staggered twice and saved himself from falling by wildly flailing his arms to keep his balance.

Desperately Dave kept going. He resisted the urge to look back. Turning his head, even for an instant, would throw him off his stride. He labored up a hill and then trotted down its far side, lurching and sliding in the wet snow. Ahead of him stretched a broad rolling valley, almost clear of forest, but heavily patched by thickets of shrub oak and evergreen bushes. As he entered the valley, a big buck rose from its bed in a thicket, stared at Dave for a second, snorted in alarm, and bounded away with its white flag flashing. An instant later a doe, heavy with fawn, burst from another thicket and followed the buck.

Dave struggled on, thinking how easy it would be to escape if he had the speed of that big buck. He fell for the first time when he was well into the valley. He scrambled to his feet and took his first look over his shoulder. They weren't in sight, and there was a quarter of a mile between him and the rise they would come over. He still had a chance. Maybe they were almost as tired as he was.

He'd gone another hundred yards when he heard them. First it was a broken scream that sounded faintly. That yell of triumph was followed by others. He looked back. They were strung out on the hill, all four of them, all Indians, and running effortlessly, it seemed to Dave. He took another look in spite of the danger of falling. The second man in line was sprinting, going by the leader as easily as if the other were standing still. Dave knew the strategy. Now that he was in sight, they'd push him to the limit. One after another of them would sprint, letting the others come at a normal run. Dave would be run into the ground trying to stay ahead of the leader's pace.

He went on another hundred yards before he looked back again. The sprinter was much closer now. When he saw Dave looking at him, he screamed once, a brief, choked whoop of victory.

Dave gave up. He stopped running and turned. He stood on trembling legs, gasping for breath, with no weapons but his clenched fists, and his arms felt so weak he didn't think he could lift them in defense.

He was desperate. The leading Indian had drawn his tomahawk. Dave realized he would have no chance to wrest it away before the blade struck him down, but he was going to try. It was all he could do.

As soon as the Indians saw that he had abandoned hope of escaping, they slowed down. The leader swung in a wide circle off the trail to the right. The second man went to the left. The last two came straight toward Dave. They all brandished tomahawks.

Dave thought they planned to circle him before they rushed him. He faced one of them after another, trying vainly to watch them all at once, to meet the first on-slaught. They completed the circle, then stood there watching him. Their chests were heaving, and their mouths were open to suck air. One of them crouched and began to rub his legs briskly.

"Come on!" Dave said wildly. "Get it over with."

One of the Indians took a step forward. His tomahawk was at his side. His face was a grotesque mask of black, yellow, and vermilion stripes. The paint cracked as he peeled his lips back from his teeth in an ugly grimace. It took Dave a moment to realize that the man was smiling. He said something that Dave couldn't understand. It was only a few words, apparently in English, but Dave couldn't make it out. He shook his head puzzledly.

The Indian tried again, very slowly this time. "No kill," he said. "Thayendanegea say no kill."

Thayendanegea was Brant's Mohawk name. Dave nodded slowly, trembling as the tension began to leave him. It took him a few seconds to speak. "What are you going to do with me?"

"Take Yankee back," the Indian said.

One of the other Indians spoke harshly in his own language. The spokesman grunted and looked keenly at Dave. "Yankee run good," he said. "All sit now. Eat meat. Go back."

"I won't argue," Dave said wearily.

The Indian looked puzzled. Dave tried again by simply saying, "Yes."

The Indian wasn't satisfied. "We kill if you run more. I tell you we kill." He waited for an answer.

Dave nodded. "All right. I won't try it again."

"Good. Sit down. Eat. You run good. Seneca run better."

All four were Senecas. They were dressed in buckskin leggings, high winter moccasins, and jackets of animal hide with the fur inside for warmth. Their heads were shaved, and three of them wore brass swivels in their scalp locks, from which dyed turkey feathers dangled. The fourth man had his scalp lock bound by a silver shoe buckle. All but the man with the buckle were lean and wiry. He was a giant, taller and broader than any Indian Dave had ever seen. His painted face cracked into what was obviously a grin when he saw Dave looking at him. He nodded his head and kept grinning grotesquely.

Dave spoke to the leader. "When did you find out I was gone?"

The Indian obviously didn't understand. Dave repeated the question slowly. This time the leader looked at the big Indian, as if inviting him to interpret. The giant spoke in a surprisingly soft voice and in much better English than the other Indian had used.

"Brant came to us last night," he said. "Maybe moon was there," he added, pointing to the sky to indicate that the time had been about midnight. "Brant said, 'Yankee soldier Harper is gone.' He said, 'Run after him. Bring him back. Do not hurt him. Son of my old friend.'" The giant laughed. "Brant knew I will not hurt Nat Harper's son. Nat Harper was my old friend too."

Dave was surprised to hear that Brant had issued such orders, for he supposed that to the Indians a fleeing captive was fair game. Evidently the Mohawk chief had determined that Nat Harper's son should come to no harm while in his hands. And now this big Indian had also spoken of Nathan Harper with affection.

Dave thought he knew who this big warrior was. He remembered a winter long before the war, before his father had bought the land in Cherry Valley. In those days Nathan Harper was a trapper and trader, and the year that Dave recalled, his father had been gone from fall until spring on a fur-trading venture among the Seneca villages in the west. When he returned, he told his family about a giant Indian youth who had followed him about like a pet bear. "You must be Tommy Infant," Dave said to the big man.

His answer was another rolling laugh. "You right, Harper. Tommy Infant, me. Your father make me learn English. I work for him. Plenty sweet-drops." The Indian rubbed his belly. "Harper give sweet-drops every day. Other Indians want whiskey, not sweet-drops. Too bad. Harper gets no furs. Seneca want whiskey. No whiskey, no furs. Too bad."

Dave knew it was true. His father had always refused to buy furs from the Indians with whiskey, as other traders did. That was one of the reasons why he had quit the Indian trade to farm his land in Cherry Valley. Other men had grown wealthy by furnishing cheap whiskey to the Indians, but Nat Harper, by refusing to do so, had failed to make a living for his family.

"I won't take more than I need for the chiefs and sachems," he used to say, "and maybe a drop or two to warm myself on a cold winter's night. There's not many things worse that your eyes can light on than a hull village full of drunk Injuns."

"Come, Harper," Tommy Infant said now. "We eat." He took a huge slab of greasy ox meat from his hunting bag, cut it in half, and offered Dave a share. It was tough and stringy, and there were grains of gunpowder and tobacco clinging to it. It had the taste of rancid bear's fat, but Dave chewed it with satisfaction. All the Indians were eating noisily. None of them spoke until the meal was over and they had wiped their hands on their clothing. Then the leader rose from the snow, shook himself like a dog rising from a dusty bed, and stroked the muscles of his legs. He grunted a few words in Seneca and lifted his arm toward the west.

"We go now," Tommy Infant said. "I put your coat in tree back there where you threw it. You a good runner, Harper. You can run back?"

"I'll keep up with you," Dave said.

The Indian grinned. "Make joke. No need to run now."

Dave nodded morosely. He didn't think it was funny. To have come so far and then be caught! He told himself that his failure was deserved because he had been over-confident that they wouldn't discover he was gone until it was too late to catch him. Next time, he thought, I won't stop running until I get there. Next time! I may never get another chance, he told himself bitterly.

"How far did you have to chase me?" Dave asked. "How close are we to Stanwix?"

"Huh!" Tommy Infant said, shaking his head in admiration. "You almost make it." He pointed to the eastern horizon. "Stanwix there, maybe eight, maybe ten miles."

The leader of the party uttered an explosive burst of Seneca. Tommy Infant gave Dave a gentle shove, suddenly looking fierce as he stiffened his painted features. They started westward after the leader, jogging easily.

Dave heard Tommy Infant's disgruntled voice in his ear. "You know him? Seneca name——" and there followed a string of harsh syllables that Dave couldn't catch. He shook his head.

"White man call him Hot Bread," Tommy said. "Great warrior, Hot Bread. Big chief. Give orders. Go now. Come now. Sit down now. Huh! Someday I throw him over the big falls at Niagara."

Dave couldn't help grinning. It occurred to him that all armies must be the same. The soldiers always grouse about the officers.

CHAPTER FOUR

They caught up with the war party on the third day. It was already beyond the lake country in the approaches to the Genesee River Valley.

Dave was taken directly to Joseph Brant at the head of the column, and the other prisoners stared curiously at him as he went by. Brant stepped aside when he saw Dave. There was a slight smile on his face.

"How far did you get?" he asked quietly.

"Almost all the way," Dave answered defiantly. "I was less than ten miles from Stanwix when they caught me. Another hour's start and I would have made it."

"You would have made it if we had not discovered that you were gone. I am apt to prowl the camp at night. I saw that one prisoner was missing."

"I was sure I'd have the whole night," Dave admitted.

Brant's face grew stern, and there was a cutting edge to his next words. "Don't try it again! There is a limit to my control of the Senecas. They may kill you next time."

"I'll run if I get the chance," Dave said, looking straight into Brant's angry eyes.

The Indian spoke swiftly and harshly. "You won't get the chance, even if we have to keep you tied up."

Dave didn't reply. Brant studied him coldly for a few seconds, then his anger disappeared. "You will not suffer for your trick this time, young Harper. We admire courage. All right. It's finished."

He held up his hand and called a short command in the Mohawk tongue. The column stopped marching. Brant beckoned the prisoners to him. When they were grouped before him in a half circle, he began to speak.

"We are approaching the first of the Seneca villages. Listen carefully to what I say. So far you have not been harmed or mistreated. I will do my best to see that you arrive safely at Niagara. However, to get there, we must pass through the land of the Senecas. Were any of you with General Sullivan two years ago?"

There was no response for a few seconds, and then two soldiers hesitantly lifted their hands.

Brant nodded. "You men know what Sullivan's army did to the Seneca country. You burned their villages, you destroyed their crops, you girdled their fruit trees, you polluted their water supplies—in short, you devastated their homeland. You did this to the Senecas and the Cayugas. Other Continentals burnt out the Onondaga country. I know that your Congress ordered it, but the Indians do not know it. They blame all Continentals, all Yankees.

"The destruction you caused was intended to put an end to our raids against your frontiers. General Sullivan and his five thousand men left a dead country behind them. But you men have the best reason of all to know that the raids have not ended. They have grown worse, in fact. We no longer have bases in the Seneca country, nor along the Susquehanna. We have to come all the way from Niagara. But we come, and we will keep coming until your evil rebellion is crushed!"

Brant's voice rose with the last words, and his ringing tones had their effect on the prisoners. Most of them were staring at the ground, as if they were school children being scolded by the master.

Brant's emotion left him as suddenly as it had come. When he spoke again, after a pause, his voice was calm and authoritative once more. "I tell you this because you must go through the Seneca villages, or what is left of them. Our Seneca allies are bitter. They hate all Yankees. They will demand that we give you up to them. I won't do that. My word to these warriors and the Rangers will protect you. But you must help. Offer no resistance, no matter what they do! Don't run, don't fight back, and keep calm. The warriors and Rangers will take you through. Stay close to them."

Betts lifted his hand to get Brant's attention. "What will the Indians do?" he asked.

Brant answered bluntly, "They'll beat you to death if they can. But if you stay together, close to my men, you'll not be hurt."

He ordered the prisoners to return to the column and resumed the march. Dave fell in beside Betts, who was marching with Sam Hawkins. The warm spell that had melted most of the snow had benefited the prisoners. None of them had difficulty in matching the raiders' steady pace once the snow was gone.

"What you think is likely to happen when we hit them Injun towns, Harper?" Betts asked.

"I don't know," Dave said truthfully, although he could picture the mobs that would assail them. "I suppose we'll

be all right if we do what Brant says. He's brought prisoners in before."

"I'm scared," Sam Hawkins said softly. "I'm just plain
scared. I wish I was back home to Kingston."

Sam and Betts walked along silently, probably both
thinking of their homes in the Hudson Valley. As for Dave,
he was remembering stories of the ferocity of the Indians
toward prisoners. He was worried about the treatment that
awaited them in the Indian towns. How much protection
would the Rangers and the Indians of the war party give
them? A few minutes later he realized that the answer lay
just ahead. He called for his companions' attention. "Look
ahead there," he said. "There's the first town."

The village lay at the tip of a hollow traversed by a
swift creek with brown, storm-swollen water. There were
four buildings on a rise above the creek. They were the
traditional long houses of the Six Nations, of elm-bark
construction with domed roofs. There had once been
many more buildings in the town, but they were now
heaps of fire-blackened ruins scattered on the rise. There
had been an orchard in the hollow, spreading over many
acres on both sides of the creek. Half the trees were down,
and the rest were dead or dying, each showing a strip
of white wood around the trunk where the hatchets of
Sullivan's men had girdled them. The fields beyond the
orchard, where the people of the town had once grown
corn and beans and squash and cucumbers, were now
choked with a year's growth of brush and with the refuse
of unharvested crops.

Almost all of the prisoners had been farmers before the
war or had at least lived in farm country, and they stared
curiously at the desolate land. Their experienced eyes cal-

culated the extent of the damage that had been done. Although they had heard many tales of General Sullivan's
campaign of destruction against the Six Nations, this was
their first realization of the damage that an army of almost
five thousand men could do when ordered to lay waste a
countryside. The two men among the captives who had
been with Sullivan were talking to their companions in
low voices, forgetting their own plight as they told how
they'd swept through this land two years before.

As the war party passed through the orchard and approached the high waters of the creek, the men who had
been with Sullivan lapsed into silence. All the prisoners
watched the village nervously. None of them trusted
Brant and the mixed group of Mohawks and Senecas who
were their guards. Why should one band of Indians protect them from another? How far could they trust Brant's
promise that his men would keep them from harm? They
bunched together for the feeling of security in numbers.
The Indians prodded them along impassively.

A dog in the village began to bark wildly. He was joined
by several others. They appeared from among the houses—
lean, vicious-looking mongrels that raced along the bank
of the stream, shrilling defiance at the strangers.

The leading Indians waded into the creek. The prisoners bunched together to follow them. The villagers now
came into view, running from the houses and grouping
on the rise to stare across the creek. When they saw that
the returning raiders were bringing prisoners, they swept
in a screaming wave to the stream. There were forty or
fifty of them, mostly women and children.

While the prisoners were picking their way across the
torrent, with icy water swirling sometimes to their hips,

the villagers began to attack. The women and children waded into the water, their hands full of water-smoothed rocks. They stoned the struggling captives and yelled savagely every time a missile hit its mark.

The prisoners cowered and tried to protect their heads with their arms. Some of them lost balance and sprawled in the water. A soldier named Jurgens was struck in the head by a rock the size of a duck egg, and his companions had to drag his unconscious body to the shore.

Brant's Indians, now on the bank, hurried to form a ring around the prisoners as they emerged from the water. The Rangers crossed the stream diagonally and formed a barrier that the women and children couldn't pass. The men of the village stood impassively by, offering no violence to the captives. The stoning of prisoners was women's work. Rocks continued to fly, and some men were hit, but the first savage flurry passed without anyone being seriously hurt except Jurgens.

Another attack came when the column began to move up the slope toward the village. Again it came from the women and children, who suddenly swept through the guards, carrying clubs and sharp-pointed sticks. They jabbed and beat the captives until the Rangers and Indians jostled them away. During all this uproar the dogs of the village darted here and there among the prisoners, snapping at legs and hands. Their snarling and yapping, coupled with the screaming of the women and children, made an earsplitting din.

Most of the prisoners sought only to protect themselves by hiding behind the Rangers and Brant's Indians. They offered no resistance to the stones or the clubs and spears. A man named Ellsworth was the only one to ignore Brant's

advice. A jab from a pointed stick in the hands of an Indian boy made a crimson gash in his neck. Ellsworth,
roaring with rage, shoved the boy away from him, and the
boy tripped and fell. Screaming more wildly than ever,
the women converged on Ellsworth and beat him with
clubs. He fell to the ground, bleeding and bruised.

The Rangers forced the women away with clubbed
muskets, and the attack was ended. With a tight ring of
Rangers and Indians around them, the captives were
taken into the village.

The war party halted there for its noon meal. While
slabs of ox meat were searing in the flames, Brant again
spoke to the prisoners.

"It will be worse for you when we get to Little Beard's
Town," he said. "It was a big town before Sullivan destroyed it, and some of the people have returned from Niagara to live there. Remember, no resistance! Don't put up
a fight. You saw what happened to that man," he added,
pointing to Ellsworth, who was lying half conscious on
the ground.

"Why don't you take us around the villages?" Betts
asked. "That way they wouldn't bother us."

Brant stared coldly at him. "I'm taking the direct route
to Niagara, Corporal. I'm not concerned with your wel-
fare."

"Why do they do this to us?" Betts cried passionately.
"We're just prisoners of war. We got a right to be treated
fair, ain't we?"

"You ask for fair treatment?" Brant exclaimed, his eyes
narrowing and his face growing even darker than its
normal hue. "Look around you! Look at this town, burned
to ashes. Look at these Senecas who have returned here

to try to live. If they beat you and stone you, they are making payment for what was done to their homes."

"You done the same to our towns," Betts said doggedly. "Every year since '77 you've brought your Injuns into the Mohawk Valley and burned it out."

"Your people started the war, Mr. Betts."

"We don't mistreat prisoners," Betts said. "We fight like civilized people."

Brant laughed shortly. "If you were civilized, as you say, you wouldn't fight at all. Neither would we." His tone changed suddenly, as it always did. It was a cold and level voice now, but it betrayed the fury he was repressing. "You don't mistreat prisoners, Betts? Haven't you ever heard of Lieutenant Hare and Sergeant Newberry? Your General Clinton hanged them in 1779, when they were captured on a scouting trip. They were in Ranger uniform, but he called them spies.

"None of you can deny having heard the white man's favorite saying about my people. You all know it! 'The only good Indian is a dead one.' Deny if you can that you white men have robbed us, cheated us, stolen our land, murdered us when given the opportunity." Brant stopped talking and glared at Betts. Then he seemed to collect himself. His voice was calm when he spoke again. "I see no point to arguing with a rebel and a traitor, Mr. Betts. Just remember, when we go through other Seneca villages, to follow my instructions. I will protect you to the best of my ability."

There was no further trouble in the village. Brant's Indians distributed meat to the people, whose skinny bodies and sunken faces showed the hardships inflicted by a severe winter in a land that could no longer support them. The war party took the trail again, going overland toward Little Beard's Town.

Here the scene at the first village was repeated and intensified. There were many more villagers, and while the men of the town took no part in assailing the captives, the women and children increased their ferocity in proportion to their numbers. The combined efforts of warriors and Rangers saved the captives from severe harm, but every man bore the marks of sticks and stones by the time the uproar had subsided. Dave had been apprehensive that there would be a concerted effort to wrest the captives away from the war party, to force them to run the gantlet. Certainly some of the Continentals would have been killed if they had been forced to dash between two lines of Indians armed with clubs, spears, tomahawks, and axes. Apparently, however, Brant was able to exert enough authority to prevent that.

Little Beard's Town had been one of the principal villages in the Seneca country, ruled by the man for whom it was named, one of the great warriors of his people. Now the site of the former town was covered with charred ruins of long houses. A dozen or so new buildings had been put up, each housing four or five families who had chosen to return to the Genesee River to live by the efforts of their hunters and fishermen rather than depend upon the British at Niagara for food and clothing. All the Indians were gaunt and most of them looked as if they were starving. Only a glance at the land was needed to see why. A few acres were turned over, ready for planting. The stubble and debris left from the crops of two years before covered all the rest of the land that the town had formerly

EAGLE OF NIAGARA 70

cultivated. Sullivan's men had done a thorough job in destroying harvest and seed for seasons to come.

Dave recalled how bitter the people of the settlements had always been when the Indians burned them out. Sullivan had turned the tables. It was one of the terrible results of border warfare that women and children on both sides suffered privation of the worst kind.

These Indians, Dave thought, had been homeless and starving just like the people of Cherry Valley, Schoharie, the German Flats, and the Pennsylvania settlements. Dave tried to tell himself that the Indians were not to be pitied, because they had started the raids. But in spite of himself he was moved with compassion every time he saw a sunken-eyed Indian child with the potbelly and protruding bones of malnutrition.

The party pressed on without halting in Little Beard's Town. From time to time they passed isolated Indian dwellings, where a refugee had built himself a house and tried to farm a few acres to support his family. Dave Harper remembered how his father had said that the white men on the frontier could profit by studying the farming methods of the Six Nations, telling time and again of the great fields of corn that grew in the fertile Genesee country and of the abundant harvests of vegetables that filled the Indian storage pits every autumn. There was no sign of this agricultural genius in the few cultivated acres along the trail. Both of the men who had been with Sullivan agreed that they had never seen crops as rich and abundant as those they had destroyed two years before.

"It wasn't nothin' like that scrawny stuff," one of them said as they were passing a field of dead corn left standing by the Indian who had planted it last season. "Look at it, three-four feet high. I'm telling you! I walked through cornfields where a man could get lost. Reach your arm up and you couldn't touch the tops of the stalks. We found ears of corn that your two hands, with fingers spread out, could hardly cover."

"That's right," the other man said. "And we burnt it all, or ran the horses over it, or turned a regiment into it with bay'nets. We burnt all their seed. That's why they got nothin' now."

CHAPTER FIVE

On the morning of the fifth day they entered the open country that stretched east and south of Fort Niagara. The lowlands were, for the most part, grassy plains, while the hills were dotted by sparse growths of timber and brush. There were Indian villages at frequent intervals along the trail. The houses were flimsy, misshapen structures of elm bark and poles, built as if their owners intended to stay only a few weeks and then move along. In contrast to the towns in the Genesee country, these people were obviously making no attempt to support themselves. The fertile ground was unbroken, and the people had the hangdog look of idlers who want nothing from life but the next handout.

They came alive, however, at the approach of the returning raiders. Each cluster of huts spewed forth its women and children and dogs to plague the captives. Mile after mile, the prisoners were the targets of rocks and clods, and were poked and prodded whenever the villagers managed to break through the barrier of Rangers and Indians. The men of these villages looked on with sullen hatred.

The closer they came to Niagara, the more Dave grew

discouraged at the fading prospects of escape. Deep in the heart of the Indian country, it would be almost impossible to evade pursuers even if he could manage to break away. The Indians knew all the trails and he knew none of them. There seemed no hope for anything but dreary captivity as long as the war lasted.

Almost all of the Indians living on the trail to Niagara were Senecas, Cayugas, and Onondagas. The towns of all three nations had been destroyed by the Continental Army. Bad as the condition of the people in the Genesee towns had been, the state of these Indians was far worse. They were ill clothed. The ravages of scurvy and the marks of two winters of near famine were evident.

Tommy Infant told Dave about the privations suffered by his people since the Sullivan expedition. "No seed, no tools," the big Indian said as he marched at Dave's side through a hamlet of five Seneca long houses. "Come to Niagara, all the people. They put out their hands, and they say, 'Feed us.' Colonel Bolton say, 'Go back to your villages. Hunt and fish.' They won't go. Colonel Bolton say then, 'Go to Canada. The King will send you food and seed in your new homes in Canada.' They won't go. This is their country. They stay here with hands out. They starve last winter. They starve this winter. Many die."

The conversation was interrupted by an attack of screaming women and children. The prisoners were adept by this time at protecting themselves, and these attacks were not as furious as those of previous days. These villagers hadn't the strength or the will to break through the guards.

Dave picked up the talk again when they were past the

village. "Can't Colonel Bolton bring supplies from Quebec and Montreal?"

Tommy Infant shrugged. "Bolton dead now. Drowned on the lake. Got General Powell at fort now."

"Can't he do something?" Dave asked.

Joseph Brant, who was marching near the captives, evidently had overheard some of the conversation. "Have you ever seen the St. Lawrence, young Harper?"

"No, sir," Dave answered. It was the first time he had used that title of respect, but he had decided it was proper because he knew Brant held a commission as colonel in the Indian Department of the British forces.

"It's a big river," the Mohawk said. "There are rapids that are miles long. Every bit of supplies must be brought up by bateau. Niagara is the supply post for Oswego, Fort Erie, Detroit, and Michilimackinac in the far west, as well as for itself. We need every inch in the boats for military supplies. And then the river closes up in November and stays closed until May. General Powell can do little for these poor people." He lifted his arm and swept it across the horizon to encompass the villages in sight.

"Seed doesn't take up much space," Dave said. "One boatload of seed could feed several hundred people the next year."

Brant looked at him searchingly, a slight smile on his wide mouth. "You show much concern for your enemies. Why do you care whether my people starve, especially when they beat you with sticks and pelt you with stones?"

Dave was silent for a few seconds. Through his mind flashed the memory of the flight from Cherry Valley during the raid. He saw the faces of his two younger brothers twisted with fear and his mother pushing through the snow, holding the boys' hands. He remembered how the boys had whimpered with hunger and cold. They'd had no food, shelter, or warm dry clothing for two days. "The children shouldn't have to go hungry," he said to Brant. "Something could be done for 'em."

"We do our best," Brant said. "The war comes first." He lengthened his stride and left them.

For some time there had been a noticeable vibration in the air, and now it became a distant rolling roar that rose and receded. It sounded to Dave like a far-off summer storm in which the thunder echoed and re-echoed incessantly in the mountains.

Others noticed it too. "What's that booming?" Sam Hawkins asked. "Sounds like a bunch of barrels rollin' around in a cooperage."

Tommy Infant grinned. "Niagara," he said. "Water over the falls."

They came in sight of Fort Niagara an hour later. The prisoners had expected a typical frontier post, larger than Stanwix probably, but they were not prepared for the magnitude of the scene before them. The fort itself, palisaded and bastioned, was built at the mouth of the Niagara River, at the edge of the great frozen expanse of Lake Ontario, the largest body of water most of the captives had ever seen. Many stone buildings were enclosed by the palisade, and one of them poked seven chimneys into the air. There were a dozen barracks and warehouses visible in the stockade's enclosure, but more impressive was the area on the plain around the fort. A ramshackle city was sprawled on the treeless land. There were hundreds of long houses, a few frame buildings, many storehouses, huts of all descriptions, and here and there a cluster of tents—some of them trim and military, and others grotesque in a patchwork of worn and tattered canvas. Indians by the thousands swarmed on the plain. Among them could be seen the spots of red and green color marking military jackets. Near the fort a company of redcoats was drilling on a parade ground, with several hundred Indians watching them.

Across the river, a group of long frame and log buildings stretched along a rise of ground in precise order. These were the barracks of Butler's Rangers. Beyond them were cultivated fields extending in all directions, dotted here and there by neat log cabins.

The prisoners were astonished by the scene. Dave Harper had visited the city of Albany once years ago. Surely there were at least twice as many people here at Fort Niagara than there were in the capital of New York. There must be fifteen or twenty thousand—more, if the Indians in the outlying areas were counted.

Brant sent runners ahead to the fort. The party halted at his command, and the reason for the halt was soon obvious. Drums began to roll in the fort, the sound blending in the distance with the faint roar of the falls. Three companies of red-coated soldiers came hurrying through the gates. They formed on the plain and were joined by the company that had been drilling. The long red column began marching toward the returning war party.

By this time, word of Brant's return had spread among the Indians in the sprawled city outside the palisade. Ahead of the swiftly moving British soldiers, streamed hundreds of screaming Indians, their numbers swelling every second.

Brant shouted a short order in his own language and

nodded to Captain Bradt. The Rangers and Indians again formed their usual ring around the prisoners, clubbing their muskets. The captives gathered apprehensively in the center of the ring.

This time, however, the Indians didn't try to get at the prisoners. A few stones and clods flew through the air, but most of the people stayed in a milling mob that screamed a wild tumult of threats and insults.

The British soldiers arrived and formed a solid wall around the war party. Imperturbably they shouldered the Indians out of the way when Brant gave the order to proceed. The dogs were the only breakers of the cordon. Mangy and gaunt mongrels swept through the line of red-coats, ripping and tearing at the prisoners' legs. They seemed to sense the presence of enemies, although a few of them snapped at any man, Ranger or Indian, within reach of their jaws.

Slowly the column moved across the plain through the howling crowd that now numbered at least two thousand Indians. The marks of hunger and disease were on almost every face.

At the gates of the fort the mob began to disperse, and the captives were led into the comparative quiet of the interior. The scene within the palisade was one of orderly discipline. Red-coated soldiers hurried through the streets of the fort, others were pacing the bastions on sentry duty, and still more were drilling on the small parade ground near the barracks. While the returning war party moved from the gate toward the tall building with the seven chimneys, Rangers in green coats and buckskin leggings fell into step beside it, asking questions of Captain Bradt's men. They surveyed the prisoners without comment, their cold eyes and hard faces showing no emotion. Dave Harper was reminded of the battalion of Daniel Morgan's Rifle Corps that had been stationed in the Schoharie Valley in 1779. Morgan's riflemen had the reputation of being the roughest, wildest soldiers in the Continental Army. Their outfit was feared by the British for the deadly accuracy of its long Kentucky rifles.

These Rangers of Colonel John Butler's regiment were the same breed of men—frontiersmen who could travel and fight in the roughest country, who knew Indians and their ways, who were almost Indians themselves. Dave had heard it said that one of the enlistment requirements in Butler's Rangers was that a man had to know at least one Indian language.

They had none of the stiffness and proper military bearing of the British regulars. Most of them were lean and lithe and walked with the grace of wild creatures. They gave evidence of the arrogance of elite military organizations the world over; they obviously believed themselves to be a breed apart from all others. On the journey to Niagara, Dave Harper had observed Captain Bradt's company man by man, and was inclined to accept their claim that with five such regiments stationed on the frontier the Butlers could drive the Continental garrisons out of the settlements. Even here in the drill-field atmosphere of Fort Niagara, Dave could remember with pictorial clarity the morning of the Cherry Valley raid. He had sent his mother and brothers ahead in flight, while he lay in the snow on a hilltop, looking down into the valley. He had seen those green coats sweeping in the dawn shadows toward the distant fort, and he had shivered with sudden

fear as he watched the swift, silent, and deadly figures
flow across the valley.

A group of officers and Indians stood waiting for the
war party in the courtyard of the stone building. Some
of them were dressed in Ranger uniforms, others in scarlet
coats. The Indians stood to one side, wrapped in blankets.
Brant halted his column and went forward. He shook
hands with the officers in turn, starting with a tall handsome Britisher in a splendid uniform. Dave surmised that
this was the new commander of Fort Niagara, Brigadier
H. Watson Powell. Next to Powell stood a bulky man with
saturnine features, who wore a green jacket slightly different from that of the Rangers. He scowled frequently as
Brant talked in low tones.

Dave guessed that he was one of the Johnsons—either
Sir John, Sir William's son, or Colonel Guy Johnson, the
dead baronet's nephew. The Johnsons had inherited Sir
William's lands and power but were disliked by Mohawk
Valley people for their arrogance. Since 1777, Sir John
had commanded his own corps, the Royal Regiment of
New Yorkers, which was composed mostly of loyalists who
had been tenants or employees of Sir William. Guy Johnson had succeeded to his uncle's post as His Majesty's Indian Superintendent for North America.

The other two men who were listening closely to what
Brant had to say were easily recognized by any resident
of the Mohawk Valley. They were John Butler and his son,
Captain Walter Butler, leaders of the Rangers. John Butler had been Sir William's loyal lieutenant since the days
of the old French War and had owned a great estate at
Butlersbury on the Mohawk. Since the battle of Oriskany

in 1777, he and his raiders had been the most active of the King's forces on the long frontier.

His son Walter, who before the war had been one of the most promising young attorneys in Tryon and Albany counties, with a limitless future before him, now was hated and feared in every frontier settlement from Schenectady to Fort Pitt because he had led the Indians and Rangers against Cherry Valley. He had no defenders on the rebel side, although Dave knew that there was ample evidence that he had had nothing to do with the massacre. He and his Rangers had been attacking the fort while the Indians went wild in the village. Walter Butler had stopped the murders as soon as he could dispatch Rangers to the town—some distance from the fort—but his name was blackened forever because he had been in command of the expedition.

In physical appearance the Butlers did not fit their reputation as fiends and monsters. John Butler was a man of middle height, with a sharp face, keen eyes, and iron-gray hair. He looked like a man born to authority. His son was tall and slender, with pale even features and black hair. His face seemed permanently cast in serious lines, and Dave wondered if Captain Butler ever smiled.

General Powell said a few casual words when Brant had finished his brief report, and strolled over to inspect the captives. With a trace of humor twisting his aristocratic face he spoke to them in clipped British tones.

"Baron Steuben, I am told, has made an army of you farmers. I fail to see it." The trace of humor vanished. His words snapped sharply. "Stand at attention!"

Startled, the Continentals obeyed. They were a sorry sight: unshaven, grimy with wood smoke and dirt from the journey, and many of them with torn and ragged uniforms. Most of them showed fear of their fate in their anxious eyes and strained faces. They realized that their future would now be settled, and although they obeyed General Powell's command with the automatic reaction of well-drilled veterans, their misery showed plainly.

Powell walked down the line, studying each man. Smiling, he shook his head. He looked across at John Butler. "All right, Colonel. You may speak to them. I doubt if you can persuade them, and even if you could, I don't think they'd qualify."

Colonel Butler came forward. His voice was harsh and swift, and he punctuated his words frequently by emphatic repetition. "You men are rebels. You are traitors to the King. Traitors! We offer an opportunity for you to escape the certain punishment that will come to you when your rebellion is crushed. Crushed, I say! You may volunteer now for service in the Rangers. Good uniforms, good food, and the highest rate of pay in the British Army. You will serve a just cause. A just cause! Any of you who enlist with us will serve a few months of probation. Then you will become full-fledged Rangers. All who wish to enlist, step forward. Captain Butler will sign you on the spot. Step forward!"

A wave of uneasiness went through the line of prisoners but was gone as instantly as it had come. Not a man moved. Colonel Butler walked down the line, looking into each man's face, then returned to his former position. "The King's pardon for you men," he said sharply. "Take two steps forward!"

The Continentals stood rigidly in line.

"All right," Butler said. "You prefer a cold, damp

prison." He turned to Powell and the bulky man. "They're all yours."

Powell nodded, smiling as if to say, "I told you so." He looked at his companion. "Colonel Johnson?"

Johnson then addressed the prisoners. "You men were captured by Colonel Brant and his Indians. According to our system here at Niagara, the Indian Department of His Majesty's Government will purchase you from your captors. Then you will be treated as regular prisoners of war, subject to imprisonment until you are exchanged. First, do any of you prefer to remain with your Indian captors?"

He smiled frostily when there was no answer from any of the prisoners. "All right. I will now buy you out of captivity. You will be held here at Fort Niagara by the provost marshal until the St. Lawrence is open to navigation. Then you will be sent to Quebec to be imprisoned until you are exchanged to your own army. The post jailers will explain the rules of the jail to you. See that you obey them."

At these words Dave was relieved that Brant had indeed kept his word to see them safe to Niagara without harm from the Indians. Evidently there was no reason now to fear the Indians any longer. The Continentals were to be regular prisoners of war, and Guy Johnson had held out the prospect of exchange. Things didn't look so bleak. Dave glanced at the other prisoners. They were whispering excitedly to each other, and the anxiety was gone from their eyes.

Joseph Brant said a few words in Mohawk to Guy Johnson, who scowled, nodded, and answered in the same language. They evidently came to some agreement after a few more words. Johnson went into the stone building and returned shortly, followed by several civilians who staggered under heavy loads of blankets, food, muskets, odds and ends of clothing, and other commodities. The civilians went back into the building for more goods. These were piled on the ground before the war party. The warriors eyed them with excited speculation, but they didn't touch any of the piles.

Johnson crossed to the row of blanket-wrapped Indians who had gathered upon the arrival of Brant and his men. They listened impassively while Johnson's heavy voice harangued them in Mohawk. Each of them made a short speech in answer. When they had all spoken, Johnson waved to the piles of merchandise. Slowly and solemnly the Indians in blankets, who Dave supposed were chiefs and sachems, went to the gifts and inspected them. They all nodded in turn after the inspection. The warriors of the war party then rushed forward and began the distribution.

All the while, the prisoners had been standing at attention. Now a squad of British regulars came to take them to their prison. Colonel Johnson, who had been talking to Brant, interrupted. "David Harper," he called, "step out of ranks."

Startled, Dave took a step forward. Johnson scowled at him. "You are given into Colonel Brant's custody, Harper. You'll stay here at his request rather than go to Quebec. It won't affect your exchange. We are in constant touch with Quebec. When the others go through, you will too."

"I'd rather stay with the others, sir," David said firmly.

"You have no choice, Harper," Johnson rumbled. "You are Colonel Brant's prisoner."

"I want to protest, sir," Dave said. "I have the right——"

"Silence!" Johnson cried. "You'll do as we say."

Dave said no more. He wondered what this new development could mean. What did Brant want of him? He thought of the long, arduous journey between Niagara and Quebec. When the other prisoners were exchanged from Quebec, would Johnson's promise be kept—would his own exchange come through at the same time?

The other prisoners were marched away. The Indians dispersed with their rewards, and the Rangers and the British regulars were dismissed. Brant walked over to Dave and put his hand on the young man's shoulder.

"You'll be much better off, David," the Indian said. "The jail is damp and the food is bad."

"I'd rather be with my friends," Dave said coldly. "You're wrong if you think you're doing me a favor, sir."

Brant smiled. "We won't try to make a King's man of you, David. And I think you'll learn that we're not the demons and monsters that some of your people think we are. This way is better. It may be two or three years before your exchange is granted."

"What do you want with me, sir?" Dave asked uneasily.

"Well, David, let's say I do this for the sake of your father. Believe me, I held him in great esteem. One thing would help in this arrangement, David. Will you give me your parole, your word that you will not try to escape?"

"No, sir," Dave said, looking steadily into the Indian's dark eyes. "I'll run the first chance I get."

"We'll see that you don't get it." Brant smiled. "Come along. I'll take you home with me."

CHAPTER SIX

Joseph Brant lived in a small frame house a few miles upriver from the fort. His dwelling was built on a wooded promontory overlooking the river on one side and a brushy plain dotted with Indian habitations on the other. The falls were not far distant, and only strong winds blowing off Lake Ontario could muffle their dull roar.

The Indians who lived near Brant were mostly Mohawks and Tuscarora refugees from the upper Susquehanna, where their villages had been burned by troops from the Schoharie Valley. The Mohawks and Tuscaroras were good farmers, who were now tilling land ceded to Sir William Johnson many years before by the Seneca nation. Their farms and stock were better than any Dave had seen since entering the Indian country, and it was evident that the breadth of acreage that each farmer had under cultivation was sufficient to feed several families.

Brant seemed to divine Dave's thoughts as they climbed the slope toward his house. He stopped and looked back across the plowed fields on the plain. "If all the nations would do what my few Mohawks have done for themselves, there would be no food problem at Niagara."

"Where did the seed and tools come from?" Dave

asked, remembering Brant's description of the difficulties of bringing supplies up the St. Lawrence.

"The men went to Canada for the seed," Brant answered. "They traveled by canoe instead of the army's bateaux. As for the tools, our blacksmith made them."

"The Mohawks aren't starving then," Dave said.

"Not starving," Brant admitted. "But they give so much of what they produce to the other nations that they have little to spare."

Brant took Dave to the far side of the slope, facing upriver. They came through a stand of hemlocks to a rock ledge that overlooked the broad river. In the distance Dave saw the majestic falls, shrouded in mist but unmistakable in its splendor and power. He was awed by the grandeur of the sight. He had heard tales of Niagara's mighty torrent from men who had been out there in the French War—his father had tried to tell him how massive the great wall of falling water was—but he had never really believed that the stories were not exaggerations. Now his throat contracted and his breath came quickly. He stared for a long time at the tremendous cataract, feeling suddenly humble before the wonder of nature.

Brant said something in a soft voice. Dave looked at him. The Indian was smiling.

"I didn't hear you, sir."

"I spoke in Mohawk, David. I called the falls by the name the old people gave it. The Voice of Our Fathers."

"I've never seen anything like it."

"Be careful if you go there in the warm weather. There are thousands of rattlesnakes in the rocks around it. Now let's go to the house."

Dave expected to find Brant's family living in a long

house in the Indian manner. He was wrong. Brant's wife
and children were in Canada, sent there two years before,
when Sullivan's army was threatening Niagara. The exception was his son Isaac, a tall, handsome youth two or
three years younger than Dave, perhaps seventeen or
eighteen.

The only other person living with Brant was his sister
Molly, the widow of Sir William Johnson. She was an alert,
vigorous woman of middle age, with black plaited hair
and a dark pleasant face whose strong features closely
resembled her brother's. She wore deerskin clothing—
jacket, skirt, leggings, and moccasins—intricately beaded
and fringed. In the days when Sir William was alive, she
had been commonly known as "the dark Lady Johnson,"
but now Brant introduced her to Dave simply as "my sister, Miss Molly." She spoke English almost as well as
Brant did, having no trouble with personal pronouns, as
most Indians did. She greeted David calmly and pleasantly with the remark that she had heard much of his
family in the peaceful days before the war. She asked
Joseph a few brief questions about his expedition and
went into the lean-to kitchen of the house to prepare a
meal.

Brant then began to talk to his son in the Mohawk
language, leaving Dave to look around him. He had expected an Indian dwelling, or at best a rude frontier home
with no comforts or conveniences. The big room they were
in, however, which had a sleeping cubicle at either side,
flanking the fireplace in the wall on the north side, was
luxurious by any frontier standard. The floor was of wide
boards, sanded to a smooth whiteness, and the walls were
finished in milled lumber. There were two upholstered

chairs, a maple table delicately made and polished to a high gloss, with chairs to match, and there were fine china dishes on a sideboard. Two pictures were hanging on the wall opposite the fireplace. One was a good painting of Sir William Johnson, done in the late years of his life; the other was a print of Joseph Brant, showing him in full Mohawk ceremonial dress, looking young and handsome. Dave didn't know much about art and artists, but he knew that the man who had done that painting of Brant was an artist of great talent.

He was studying the picture with interest when Brant spoke to him. "It was painted in London in the first year of the war, David. Sir George Romney asked me to sit for him." Brant laughed. "I was the rage of London that year. I was presented at court and went to all the fashionable parties. I played at the best gaming clubs. I have often wondered since which Joseph Brant intrigued them more—the well-dressed gentleman from our American colonies or the savage Indian chief in his wilderness finery. I think the latter."

While his father was talking, Isaac Brant was staring openly at Dave Harper. The young Indian's face showed hostility and scorn. Dave returned the stare with a level gaze. He could see that he was going to have trouble getting along with Isaac. He wished that Brant had never brought him here but had let him share the discomforts of the jail with his fellow prisoners. Dave noticed that Brant was watching them while he talked. Undoubtedly he had seen the flash of hostility that had passed between the young men.

"Isaac," Brant said equably, "David is the son of an old friend of mine. He is our prisoner, but he is to be treated as a member of this household until we have word that he is to be exchanged. You and he can share sleeping quarters. Miss Molly will give him his blankets and any clothing he needs."

Isaac nodded coldly. "I understand," he said, speaking English perfectly.

Brant looked at his son with a speculative smile on his rugged face. "He intends to escape at the first opportunity. It will be your job to see that he doesn't."

Isaac's lips curled back from his strong white teeth in a brief smile. "You mean that he will be my prisoner?"

"That's not the word I had in mind. You will be companions and you will share the work here."

Isaac turned abruptly to his father. His face clouded and his voice was angry. "I will not be companion to a rebel. I will guard him, yes. And if he tries any rebel tricks, I'll make him wish he hadn't! But I will not be friends with him."

Brant spoke briefly and sternly in Mohawk. Isaac gave him a short reply and stared sullenly at Dave. Again he said a few words.

"You will have to agree on that with him," Brant said. He turned to David to explain. "Isaac wants to know if you are to be tied up every night. He says if you're not, he'll never be able to sleep."

Dave saw no reason to reply. They'll have to figure out their own guard detail, he thought. There's no reason why I should help 'em.

"He will not give his parole," Brant said to his son. "Perhaps you have a suggestion, Isaac?"

"I have," Isaac said coldly. "Take him back to the fort and put him in a cell with the rest of the rebels."

"You will both do what I say!" Brant said sternly. "And I say he stays here. I don't blame David for thinking about escaping. He's a prisoner, and all prisoners worth their salt think about getting away. We'll need an arrangement of some kind, though. Will you give your word, David, that you'll stay put between sunset and sunup, so that both you and Isaac can get some sleep?"

Isaac glared at David and said a few words in Mohawk. Brant's anger burst forth again.

"Rebel or not, if he gives his word, his word is good," the chief said swiftly. "At any rate, you are responsible for him. Work it out between you."

"Yes, sir," Isaac said with ill grace, turning his back contemptuously on Dave.

Directly after their meal of baked trout and corn-meal cakes, Brant returned to Fort Niagara. He rode a magnificent chestnut horse that Isaac saddled and led from the small barn behind the house. Dave was continually observing new factors in Brant's life that surprised him. Such a horse would have graced the stables of any of the landed gentry in the Mohawk Valley.

When Brant was gone, Isaac spoke directly to Dave for the first time. His words were cold and scornful. "Do you want to promise, as my father said? I don't care if you do or not."

"What will happen if I don't?"

"I will tie you hand and foot every night," Isaac said with an air of satisfaction.

Dave didn't take to the idea of sleeping in bonds. He hadn't wanted to come here in the first place, to live with the family of an enemy leader, but since he was here and would likely stay, he might as well make the best of it.

"All right," he told Isaac. "As long as you're guarding me, I won't try to get away between darkness and dawn."

"If I were you, I wouldn't try it any other time, either," the young Indian said. "You'd be back here in two hours, or else you'd be dead. This is Seneca country, and they don't like rebels any more than I do. Sometimes they burn prisoners," Isaac said deliberately, watching Dave for the effect of his words.

Dave had his own thoughts on how far he could get if he ever had the chance to go, but he didn't see any point in useless argument with Isaac. He kept quiet.

"One thing more," Isaac said. "As long as I have to spend my time with you, I want you to take off that blue coat."

Dave looked down at his worn and ripped uniform jacket. He was carrying his blanket coat over his arm. "It's all I have to wear," he said, wondering for a moment what was wrong with it.

"I'll give you a hunting shirt," Isaac said. "I don't want to be reminded that you're a rebel every time I look at you."

Dave gave vent to the anger he had so far controlled. "I didn't want to come here! I'd rather go to the prison with my friends. I don't want anything to do with Indians who make war on women and children!"

Isaac's face twisted in rage, and with an attack as savage as it was sudden, he launched himself at Dave, fingers hooked to grab his throat. Dave stepped back and raised his fists to protect himself. He jabbed his right hand in a short straight blow to Isaac's jaw. The Indian's head snapped back. He grunted and charged in again. Dave tried to rely on his fists to carry the attack, but Isaac was an accomplished wrestler, like most Indians, and he evaded the punches that Dave threw. They grappled, and Dave was thrown on his back almost instantly. His breath was knocked from him, but he tried to struggle to his feet. With a savage cry Isaac was on him, groping for his throat. They rolled over and over on the packed earth, and Dave was hard put to make his superior strength tell over the Indian's sinewy agility. Dave knew he was in real danger. Isaac wasn't just letting out his anger; he was trying to throttle, gouge, bite, and kick. With a sudden summoning of strength Dave threw the young Indian from him and scrambled to his feet. Crouching, with blazing eyes, Isaac put his hand to his belt. He pulled out a hunting knife.

Dave eyed him warily, stepping backward. "Give me a knife," he panted. "I'll fight you."

Isaac took a step forward and then another, raising the knife. Dave waited, ready to spring. His mouth was dry and his breathing was labored. He knew he would have only one chance to get the knife away. The Indian could strike as swiftly as a snake. Suddenly, just as Dave sensed that Isaac was tensing to come at him, there was a blur of motion at the door of the house, and then Miss Molly was beside her nephew, holding the wrist of his knife hand and shouting angrily in Mohawk. Slowly Isaac relaxed. He shrugged off Miss Molly's restraining hand and put the knife back in his belt.

"All right," he said harshly. "I am finished. Miss Molly is right, rebel. You are my father's prisoner, not mine. I have no right to kill you."

They spent the rest of the afternoon in hostile silence. They were working two yoke of oxen at hauling stones from a cleared and plowed field at the base of the slope. Isaac was not nearly so competent as Dave in handling the oxen, and he spent most of his time vainly trying to make them respond to his commands, while Dave quietly hauled three times as many loads on the flat stone boats.

It surprised Dave that a war chief's son should be given menial farming chores that he obviously thought were below his dignity, but Dave supposed that all the Mohawks worked in their fields when they weren't away with war or hunting parties. As for himself, Dave relished the work. He'd been in the army too long without the chance to turn his hand to farm work. As the afternoon went along, he would have forgotten that he was a captive, except for Isaac's hostility, so pleasant was the routine of doing something useful on the land once more.

They finished the field before sunset and returned to the house on the hill to find a good supper waiting for them. It was some kind of stew, mostly composed of meat, corn, and beans. Isaac ate without conversation, but Miss Molly pleasantly asked Dave how he liked the food.

"It's very good," he said. "I've been wondering what kind of meat it is, ma'am."

"You like it," she said, smiling. "I'm glad you do."

Isaac looked up without expression. His dark eyes flashed from Dave's bowl, which was already empty, to Dave's puzzled face. "It's dog meat," he said evenly. "Haven't you heard that all savages eat dogs?"

Dave felt his stomach twist at the words, but he kept his face straight. After all, meat was meat, no matter what the animal. "So that's what it is," he said. "It tasted fine."

Miss Molly laughed. "That's an old joke of Sir William's,

David. Back at Johnson Hall, whenever we had guests—
people from Albany or New York—he would always com-
pliment me loudly when the meal was over on the ex-
cellent taste of the puppy we had just eaten. This is goat
meat. Joseph brought it back from Montreal during the
winter. The Frenchmen in Canada raise many goats."

"I am sure that Harper thinks we eat dogs," Isaac said
bitterly. "When he gets back among his own people, he'll
tell them all about it. He'll call me and my father 'buck
Injuns' and call you a squaw."

"You had better hold your tongue," Miss Molly said
sharply. "Your father will be angry when I tell him you
attacked David with a knife. Don't make it any worse."

"You don't have to tell my father about the fight," Isaac
said proudly. "I'll tell him." He left the table after casting
a malevolent look at Dave.

It would be wise, Dave decided, to avoid the occasion
for argument with Isaac. He thought he could understand
why Isaac so obviously hated him. He'd feel the same if
he were in the young Indian's position. The Mohawks
were exiled from their homeland, probably never to return, and the rich valley that they had owned for hundreds of years was now given over to farmers who hated
Indians.

Brant didn't come home for supper, but he arrived later
in the evening. Dave thought it highly incongruous to see
an Indian war chief take off his cloak and handsome
jacket, kick his moccasins aside, and relax in shirt sleeves
in one of the upholstered chairs beside the great fireplace.
Miss Molly brought him a pipe and tobacco, and he was
soon puffing in quiet contemplation of the cheerful fire,
like any frontier farmer after a hard day in his fields. It

was difficult to reconcile the knowledge that the Mohawk had set fire to the long frontier with this scene of Brant at peace.

He wasn't at peace long, however. To Isaac's credit, the young Indian told his father exactly what had happened during the fight with Dave, and he admitted he had drawn his knife with the intention of using it. Brant heard the explanation in silence, while his eyes were fixed on his son's face.

When Isaac had finished his brief report, Brant turned loose a tongue-lashing such as David had never heard before. It didn't last more than a minute; Brant was evidently sure of his discipline. He promised his son swift and stern punishment if there were any more fights between him and Dave. Isaac took the dressing-down in silence. At its end, he nodded to his father and resumed his place at the table with Miss Molly. Brant looked at Dave, who was sitting quietly on a bench in one corner of the room, waiting to be shown where he was to sleep.

"There will be no more fights, David," Brant said abruptly. "Whether you start them or he does, the punishment will be the same. Do you understand?"

"Yes, sir," Dave said.

"I know that Isaac started this one, and I also know that you fought to defend yourself. Next time there will be no excuse. Is that clear to both of you?"

The two young men answered that it was.

"All right, then. It is finished," Brant said, returning to his contemplation of the fire.

Miss Molly and Isaac, sitting together at the table, were engaged in an occupation that surprised Dave. In spite of his father's many stories about life among the Indians, which had prepared Dave to find them well accustomed to civilized ways, it was somewhat disconcerting to him to see Isaac and Miss Molly poring over several copies of months-old English newspapers by the light of flickering candles. He didn't think it remarkable that they could read, considering their background, but he was confounded by the picture of domesticity. They might have been an ordinary farm family in Schoharie or Cherry Valley or the Mohawk settlements, instead of full-blooded Indians living on the edge of the wilderness.

The air of comfort in the neat room with its curtains around the small glass windows and the pictures on the walls reminded Dave of the Harper house at Cherry Valley. He supposed the weeds and brush had now covered up the charred timbers of the foundation. Had the chimney, which his father had taken such pains with, stood through the fire? Dave sighed inaudibly. Cherry Valley was far away and long ago. Someday, of course, he would go back and rebuild the cabin, turn the plow again into the fallow fields, take his ax to the forest that remained to be cleared, build barns and granaries, chicken coops and woodsheds. There would be so much to do! After the war, though, the boys would be old enough to help, and his father had always said his mother was as good a hand around a farm as any man. He even allowed himself to think that Hannah might be there. If she is, Dave told himself, I'll build the finest house in the valley. Glass windows like these, and pictures on the walls, a puncheon floor, and big stone fireplaces. But no—it was too much to expect. Hannah would have forgotten him. How long would the war last—a year, two, or maybe three?

Dave supposed he might even get to like it here with Brant if Isaac didn't make it too difficult. Certainly Brant tried to be kind to him. If the farm work kept up, he'd drive himself so hard that he wouldn't have time to worry about his family or about Hannah. By the light and warmth of the fire, he found himself deciding that he'd do his utmost to make the most of a bad situation, but nonetheless he wished that he were in prison with Betts and the others.

Miss Molly occasionally read aloud an item from the London newspapers about the war in America, written with such obvious ignorance or disregard for fact that Dave wondered if any of the English people who read the papers believed such nonsense. It seemed to him that one of the main reasons why the colonies had finally taken the drastic step of rebellion, and why they must eventually succeed in establishing their independence, was that no one in the British Government had ever bothered to learn anything of the geography of America, of its resources, or of the character of its people. The King's ministers persisted stupidly and stubbornly in ignoring factual information about America and Americans.

Joseph Brant echoed David's thought when he suddenly said at the end of one of Miss Molly's items, "Read me no more of that drivel, Molly. We ask them for troops and they send us old newspapers that talk of victories that exist only in their minds. We tell them we need five regiments of trained woodsmen, and they send us one company of Hessians. They tell us to use the Indians! All the King's ministers should have been with us against Sullivan. The first time he fired a three-pounder, the Indians started to break.

"We ask for the material to build barracks and houses, and they send us a hammer and a keg of nails. We ask for competent generals, and they send us drillmasters. I have long been weary of London's blunders."

He jumped to his feet and began to pace before the fire. Miss Molly, speaking Mohawk in a soothing voice, said a few words, following him anxiously with her eyes.

"Yes," Brant said, "you're right. It would have been different if Sir William had lived. All of New York would be in our hands. New England would have long since surrendered against a full-scale frontier attack. Even the most stupid of the King's ministers, Lord Germain, couldn't throw away a victory in America, as he has been doing, if he had Sir William Johnson to plan it for him."

Isaac spoke up sharply. "We aren't losing, sir."

"We're not winning, either. And we'll never win so long as Washington is allowed to fight and run away, time after time, while our generals don't even bother to chase him."

The fierceness of Brant's eyes as he spoke, the angry pride on his face, and the grace of his lithe body put David in mind of an eagle he had once seen on exhibition in Schenectady. To be sure, the eagle had been caged in a slatted wooden crate that permitted it no freedom of motion, and its plumage was ruffled and dirty. But the wild look in its glaring eyes, the indomitable power of its great body, and the savage beak and talons demanded awe and respect from all who gazed at it.

Dave had been fascinated by the mighty bird. He had stood before its cage for the better part of an hour, bound to stare in boyish wonder into the unblinking ferocity of its eyes. He would always remember the wild urge that had come upon him to rip the cage apart and set the eagle free. Ever after, when he saw an eagle soaring in the sky, he had watched it with that same wonder at its power, its pride, and its grace.

He remembered the eagle now as he watched Joseph Brant. The comparison brought home the reason for the terror the Indian inspired on the frontier. Like the eagle, he came out of the wilderness, striking swiftly with no warning but a savage scream, while his victims huddled together for safety, hoping that the ruthless attack would not fall upon them.

Of course it was at best a physical comparison, Dave thought, because in these past few days the Mohawk chief had demonstrated the high human qualities of friendship, kindness, and compassion.

Brant's anger vanished as suddenly as it had come, and he sat before the fire again, refilling his clay pipe. He spoke to Isaac at length in Mohawk, and Dave realized that they were talking about him. He noticed that the young Indian's dark unfriendly eyes turned in his direction from time to time.

Brant nodded finally. He looked pleasantly at Dave. "Isaac doesn't like to admit it, David, but he tells me you are a farmer. He says you can make the oxen do everything but stand on their heads for you."

Dave was surprised that Isaac had given a fair account of their work together. It would be difficult to get along with Isaac, but at least it seemed unlikely that he would resort to underhanded ways to strike at Dave. Evidently the young Mohawk was honest and truthful.

"They're good animals," Dave said to Brant. "It's not hard to work a good team."

Isaac's face darkened with anger, and Dave realized

that he had made a mistake. Brant's next words made it clear that he had.

"Isaac has told me time and again that the oxen are stupid and lazy, and now you praise them. One of you is wrong." Brant looked quizzically from one to the other. Neither of them answered.

"Do you like farming, David?" Brant asked.

"I do. Very much."

"Then we'll keep you at work with Isaac. We need every farmer we can get."

Dave hesitated before answering, but when he did his voice was firm. "I'd rather go to Fort Niagara jail."

"Why?"

Again Dave paused, this time to choose his words carefully in order to avoid rousing Brant's anger. "I don't think you have any right to ask me to raise food for you. I was sworn into the army to fight you, not to help you."

Brant nodded seriously. "I see your point, but I can answer it. You won't be helping our soldiers. All the food you raise outside the needs of this family will go to Indian women and children who have no men to provide for them."

"Are you giving me a choice?" Dave asked. "Farming or jail?"

"You're a prisoner, David," Brant said sharply. "You'll do as I say. However, I want you to understand that you're not breaking your oath of allegiance by helping us in the fields."

If he was given no choice, there was no point in objecting further, so Dave nodded shortly. "All right. I'll do it," he said.

"Good," Brant said. "The first job I want you two to

take on is clearing some of those trees on the slope. I looked at the fields today. When the leaves come out on those trees, they'll shade half the field you were clearing the stones out of. Corn won't grow in the shade."

The next day Dave and Isaac took double-bitted axes to the bottom of the slope, where Isaac, with grim distaste for the work ahead, began to hack at the nearest tree. Dave watched him for a minute or two, until Isaac suddenly looked up and said angrily. "You'd better get to work. I can't do it all."

"No," Dave said evenly, "you sure can't if you're going to do it that way."

"Listen to me, Harper! You do your work and I'll do mine. My father said to clear the trees, and the sooner we get at it, the sooner it will be done."

Dave didn't say anything else. If Isaac intended to girdle all the trees and let them fall where they would, Dave couldn't stop him.

Isaac went back to his chopping, while Dave moved some distance away. He studied the rows of trees and sighted along a dozen in a north-south line. He intended to teach Isaac a lesson. He'd drop ten or twelve trees in the time it took the Indian to fell two.

Dave walked along the row of trees he had selected, marking them with his ax to indicate where they should be notched, until he reached the tallest tree at the end of the row he had chosen. They were all hickories, with straight trunks and bunched limbs at the top. The last tree was the trigger. Dave studied its trunk and branches and walked back along the row to the first tree he had marked. His ax began to swing rhythmically. He cut a deep notch into the trunk and another on the other side.

He went from tree to tree, notching them all until he had reached the one he'd picked as the trigger. In the meantime Isaac had felled one tree and was working on his second.

Dave noticed that Isaac was stopping frequently to watch. He paid no attention to the Indian, but carefully chopped at the felling notch in the trigger tree. Occasionally he looked up to gauge the strength of the wind in the treetops. Finally he heard a sharp crack in the trunk.

"Get out of the way," he yelled at Isaac, who was standing near the row of notched trees. Isaac stepped back a few yards. He was watching interestedly.

Dave looked again at the force of the wind, which might drop the tree off the course he had planned for it. The wind had died down to a slight breeze. This was the time. He stepped forward, and his ax blade bit deeply into the trunk once, then twice, and then the third time. The tree shivered, began to lean perceptibly, and cracked again like a musket shot. Then it fell. With a crackle of breaking branches it struck the second tree in line, which snapped with a loud report and fell toward the third. One after another they went down. For a few seconds the noise was like a full-scale battle with muskets cracking and cannon booming. When it was over, a dozen trees lay in an irregular row ready for burning in the fall.

"Ai-eee," Isaac cried softly. He turned to look at the one tree he had felled and at the other he had been working on. He nodded grimly and said harshly to David, "Your way is better. Tell me what to do."

Dave hid a smile. He'd scored a minor triumph. If he kept his mouth shut, he was sure that he and Isaac would avoid any more fights.

CHAPTER SEVEN

The fields were ready for sowing, stone-free and harrowed, but the danger of a killing frost still threatened in the chill winds that blew across Lake Ontario. Dave knew it was too early to put seed into the ground. Almost daily Isaac and Dave walked two miles down-river to an abandoned Seneca village, built generations ago, where an apple orchard had been planted by the villagers. The trees were ancient and gnarled and had long since been choked by brush and scrub growth, but they were apple trees and they would put forth blossoms even if they produced no fruit.

Isaac volunteered no information, but Dave realized that the Indian was going to the apple orchard to gauge the progress of the season. When the blossoms had come and gone, it would be time to seed the fields.

There was work in plenty to do while they waited, but Isaac fretted under the burdensome chores of a farmer—building stone fences with the rocks they hauled from the fields, making tools to cultivate the crops, cutting timber for corncribs and granaries, as well as other improvements suggested by Joseph Brant.

Dave overheard Isaac discussing the farm work with

Miss Molly. He just wasn't fashioned, the young Indian said, by the Great Spirit who watched over all his children, the Mohawks, to be a farmer. Isaac said a man should never go against the design of the Lord of the world. He explained this theory at length to Miss Molly, who laughed and told him to get back to work. Dave took it all with a grain of salt, since he knew that both Joseph and Miss Molly were practicing Christians who held no brief for the old religion of the Mohawks.

The high wall of animosity between Dave and Isaac showed no signs of cracking. Sometimes two or three days went by without a word passing between them. Often during the day Isaac would leave what he was doing and go off to the house or into the woods without saying anything to Dave. Sometimes he went fishing, sometimes he went visiting friends, but frequently he would be back in ten or fifteen minutes to pick up where he'd dropped the work. During these absences Dave often thought of escaping. He was reasonably sure he could make his way through the woods and find a trail eastward to Stanwix, but he could never rid himself of the uncomfortable suspicion that Isaac was baiting him by leaving him alone. The young Mohawk might be watching him from the woods with a musket at his side, and he'd be justified in shooting an escaping prisoner.

One morning at breakfast, when Brant asked how the work was going, Isaac rebelled against routine.

"No work today," he said. "I want to go hunting."

Brant agreed. "You've been working hard. You should both have a day to yourselves."

Isaac looked surprised and displeased. "Do I have to take him too?"

Brant laughed shortly. "You're supposed to guard him. How can you keep an eye on him if you go hunting alone?"

Isaac spoke rapidly in Mohawk to his father, and although Dave had been trying his best to learn the language, he caught only a few words of what the young Indian said.

Brant replied sharply, silencing his son, and went into his sleeping quarters, an alcove partitioned by an elm-bark wall from the area used by Miss Molly. He brought out two double-barreled fowling pieces. They gleamed with silver trimmings and had delicately carved stocks of dark cherry wood. He handed one of the guns to Isaac and held up the other admiringly, showing Dave a silver plate set in the stock. Scrolled there in fine lettering was an inscription:

To Joseph Brant, Thayendanegea
From William Johnson, Bart.
Dec. 25, 1772

"Sir William gave me these guns, David," the chief said quietly. "I treasure them above all my possessions. No one has ever fired them save Isaac and myself. You may use this one to hunt with."

"Thank you, sir," Dave said, putting his hands forth to take the gun. "I appreciate it."

Brant didn't release the gun. "First, your parole, David," he said, smiling. "With this in your hands you could disarm Isaac and escape."

Dave nodded. "I give my parole while I have the gun."

"All right. Go ahead, and good hunting."

Dave and Isaac crossed the river by canoe. When they

reached the other shore, Isaac pointed to the wooded hills. "We'll go up there," he said shortly.

"You'd better tell me what we're after," Dave said.

Isaac looked puzzled. "I don't know how you white men call it," he said. "In Mohawk we say 'the bird that sounds like a drum.' Do you know what I mean?"

"Partridge," Dave said.

Isaac repeated the word. "That's what it is."

The wooded hills furnished good partridge cover, thick with clumps of evergreens and birches and plenty of brush in the blow-downs on the ridges. There was an abundance of birds, and the hunters began to flush them only a few yards from the river. The shooting was difficult because of the early foliage on the trees and brush, and it was a little late in the spring for good shooting in heavy cover.

While Isaac was far more expert at moving soundlessly through the brush, Dave was the better shot. The long light gun with its delicately fitted action came to his shoulder and fired in one smooth movement that sometimes sent partridge spinning to the ground at forty yards, a range that, for most fowling pieces Dave had ever seen, was extremely long. Twice he downed birds at that range when Isaac had already fired at them and missed.

Each of them carried a bag slung over his shoulder, hanging down between his shoulder blades. Within an hour Dave had five partridge and Isaac three. The brush was full of birds, feeding on the buds that were sprouting. Dave regretted that some of them were probably getting ready to nest, but such consideration for wild life was not common among hunters he had known. They were interested in game for the pot and cared not a whit for the hunting rights of later generations. In this case, of course, every partridge killed added to sorely depleted food supplies, so Dave's conscience did not trouble him greatly.

It was a source of constant delight to Dave to move among the trees, gun ready and senses alert, and then to be startled by the sudden whirring rush of a rocketing brown body from a brush patch. The only thing that marred the day was the memory of the many times he and his father had gone after partridge in the wooded hills above Cherry Valley.

Often three or four partridge at a time would flush from one spot of cover, and all four gun barrels would boom. When Dave hit three birds in a row while Isaac missed four, the Indian youth began to show signs of irritation.

Finally Isaac pointed to a dip in the rising hills ahead of them. "There is a valley there," he said. "It's always full of birds. We'll go there."

He moved ahead on a deer run they were following, and trotted toward the valley. A hundred yards or so along the trail a great oak had fallen, and its trunk lay directly across the run. Without a backward glance at Dave, Isaac gauged its height with his eyes and then sprinted for it.

Isaac burst into full speed a few feet from the tree trunk and, lifting his gun high before him to balance himself, he left the ground in a hurdling leap five feet high. He cleared the trunk easily. Dave started to run, not doubting that he could hurdle the trunk as easily as Isaac had.

From the other side, however, came a sudden savage roar and a strangled cry from Isaac. In the space between the trunk and the ground, Dave saw a great black body moving with incredible speed. He could see Isaac on the ground and the black figure looming over him. Dave ran swiftly, leaped to the trunk of the tree, and balanced himself there as he looked down.

A huge bear was snarling at Isaac, about to attack him. Dave lifted his fowling piece to his shoulder and fired as the bear reached the Indian. The bear screamed and lurched to one side, but it moved instantly again upon Isaac, who was trying to scramble to his feet. The bear was clawing and biting him savagely.

Dave fired the second barrel. This time the bear fell, partly across Isaac's body. The beast was up again instantly and once more seized Isaac in its grip. Dave could see blood spurting as teeth and claws tore at the young Indian.

Dave pulled his knife and leaped from the log, landing on the bear's back. The beast snapped around to face the new attack, but Dave clung to the shaggy fur with one hand and plunged his knife into the soft rolling flesh below the left foreleg. The blade penetrated and the bear stiffened. It uttered a strangled roar and snapped its head around to tear at Dave, but the blade sunk again and then a third time. The animal suddenly collapsed and fell. Dave rose panting from the dead body after repeated thrusts with his knife at the bear's heart.

He stepped to Isaac, who lay on his back, bleeding from a dozen gaping wounds in his arms and shoulders. Dave looked quickly at them and, in spite of the blood, decided that they were neither deep nor dangerous. He stripped his hunting shirt off and removed the tan linen shirt he wore under it, which he tore into strips. He bound the wounds tightly to control the bleeding. Most of the gashes could be easily bandaged.

Isaac lay with his eyes closed, breathing harshly, showing no sign of pain, but he gasped several times when
Dave pulled the bandages tight.

When the job was finished, he opened his eyes. "She
would have killed me," he said weakly. "Look there." He
pointed behind Dave, who turned to see two cubs the size
of woodchucks nuzzling at the dead body of the bear.
"That's why she went after me," Isaac said.

"Don't talk any more," Dave said. "I'll carry you back
to the canoe."

"Not the canoe," Isaac said. "Dochstadter's house is not
far away. Take me there. I'll show you the way."

Dave managed to get the young Indian to his shoulders
pickaback fashion and started with him through
the valley. It was rough walking in the brush and blow-
downs, and Dave had to choose an erratic path to avoid
obstacles. Isaac was quiet after he had given Dave whispered directions, and Dave thought he was unconscious,
judging by the limpness of his body. It was a mile and a
half to the first open country, cleared and harrowed fields
that stretched northward toward the lake. The soft, deeply
worked soil made the going even more difficult for Dave,
who lurched and stumbled over the furrows in the yielding earth.

A quarter mile distant he saw a log cabin, with other
cabins scattered in the patchwork of fields and wood lots
beyond it. The first one, he hoped, was Dochstadter's. He
headed for it.

A man stood before the cabin, looking toward Dave,
shading his eyes from the glare of the sun. He turned,
shouted something into the cabin, and ran forward. Dave
wondered if it was John Dochstadter, whom he had never

seen but knew by reputation as one of the most energetic
of the officers in the Indian Department—white men who
worked even more closely with the Indians than did
Butler's Rangers.

He saw that he was wrong, however, when the man
came toward him with a lumbering stride that carried his
huge body along with amazing speed. It was Tommy Infant, the affable giant who had been his father's friend.
Dave stopped and waited until Tommy came up to him.

"Give him to me," the Seneca commanded, taking Isaac
in his massive arms. He looked briefly at the wounds that
showed and then glanced at Dave. "Painter?" he asked,
using the frontiersman's word for cougar.

Dave shook his head. "A she-bear with cubs."

Tommy nodded heavily. "Worse than painter. Come.
Tommy will carry him to the house."

Cradling Isaac's limp body in his arms, the big Seneca
trotted across the fields. There were other people standing
near the cabin. One of them was a man in a green military jacket, one was an Indian woman, and the third was
a girl dressed in doeskin clothing.

Dave had no time to notice them as he watched Tommy
carry Isaac into the cabin, followed by the white man and
the Indian woman, who motioned that Dave was to stay
outside. The girl also remained there. After a moment she
said, speaking slowly in a low musical voice, "Sit down.
You are tired from carrying him."

He looked at her for the first time. She was a lovely
Indian girl, eighteen or nineteen years old. Her hair was
black and shining, and it hung in two long braids over
her shoulders. The shading of her skin wasn't any darker
than that of a girl of the settlements who had spent much

time in the sun, but it had a trace of the particular copper tint that distinguished Indians from sunburned white people. He could see that she wasn't of full Indian blood —her features were not cast in the typical Indian mold of high cheekbones and prominent nose. Her eyes, staring in mild curiosity at him, were almost as dark as her hair. He could feel the color rush to his face as he realized that he was thinking about her beauty.

"I am Catherine Dochstadter," she said, smiling as if she knew what was in his mind. "Lieutenant Dochstadter is my father. You are Thayendanegea's prisoner, David Harper. We have heard of you. Tell me, what happened to Isaac?"

"He surprised a she-bear with cubs," Dave answered. "She ripped him up a bit before I killed her."

At that moment Tommy Infant came bursting through the doorway. "I go for Dr. Guthrie," he called to them, heading for the trail that led upriver toward the Rangers' barracks. He was immediately followed through the doorway by the man in the green uniform jacket. He was tall and lean, with a sharp-featured, stern face. Catherine looked a great deal like him, although the lines of her face were softer.

"What happened to Isaac?" Dochstadter asked.

David told the story, omitting only the details of how he had killed the bear.

Dochstadter looked surprised. "You killed a bear with a fowling piece loaded with birdshot?"

"The shot didn't hurt her much. I had to use a knife."

Dochstadter whistled. "You jumped a bear with only a knife in your hand?"

"She was going for Isaac. I was on her before she saw me. How is Isaac now?"

"My wife will look after him until Dr. Guthrie comes. The cuts aren't bad, but I think some of his ribs are smashed." Dochstadter smiled quizzically. "How many bears have you killed with a hunting knife?"

Dave grinned. "That's the first."

Dochstadter nodded. "And the last, I should hope. Your name is Harper, isn't it?"

"That's right."

"Well, Harper, I don't think Isaac is dangerously hurt. I sent for the doctor and for Joseph. They should be here in an hour or so. Sit down and wait. My daughter will give you some food."

"I don't know if it's all right, Lieutenant, since I'm a prisoner, but I'd like to go back and get the guns. They belong to Colonel Brant. And the bear, too, if I can borrow one of your horses to pack her in."

Dochstadter looked at him sharply. "Does Joseph let you go where you please?"

"Usually Isaac is with me," Dave answered. "I'll give my parole to you, Lieutenant. I won't try to run off."

Dochstadter agreed reluctantly. "I suppose it's all right. If you're not back in two hours, I'll send Tommy after you."

"It'll be all right if I go with him, won't it, Pa?" Catherine asked.

"If he wants to take you." Dochstadter turned to Dave. "My daughter will give you some sacks for the meat and she'll show you which horses to take. I have four, but two of them are young and skittish. They'd act up if you tried to load them with fresh-killed bear meat. Give him the work horses, Catherine."

Dave and Catherine rode the two sturdy plow horses back to the wooded valley. It was a leisurely trip, since the animals could not be urged into a trot. Catherine did most of the talking on the way, telling him in detail of her trip two years before down the St. Lawrence to Quebec, where she had seen Governor Haldimand and other dignitaries and had ridden around the city in a carriage drawn by four horses—an experience she would never forget if she lived to be a hundred. She had worn a real party dress to a tea party given by Colonel Johnson for the families of Indian Department officers.

"Someday I'd like to live in a big city like Quebec," she said blithely.

Dave smiled, but he was thinking of the low opinion of Indians the Mohawk Valley gentry generally held. Even Miss Molly, he remembered, had never been accepted by Sir William Johnson's wealthy friends. Catherine would be happier among the Indians, even though her father was a white man.

She asked a question that startled him. "Why are you a rebel, David? My father says all rebels are thieves and scoundrels, but you don't look like a thief or a scoundrel."

Dave asked her question with another. "It's known to be a fact on our side that all Tories are liars and traitors. Are you a liar or a traitor?"

"Of course I'm not! That's not true. You know some of our people. You know it's not true."

"And if you knew some of ours," Dave countered, "you'd realize that they're not thieves and scoundrels."

"Oh, I wish this terrible war were over," she said

plaintively. "Then the King would give you all a pardon and we could live in peace again."

"We want no pardons from your King! We're a separate country now."

"You don't think the King will pay any attention to that foolishness, do you?"

"Ask your father," Dave said seriously. "Ask him if he really thinks your side will win this war."

"Of course he does!"

"I don't think Colonel Brant does."

She didn't answer, but glared at him angrily. Then she kicked her heels into her horse's flanks, forcing him into a lurching run. She drew well ahead of David, who didn't try to catch her but contented himself with watching in amusement as she bounced and rolled on the old nag. She knew the forest well, and he lost sight of her when she disappeared into it. When he reached the huge log where the bear lay, she was already dismounted and had tethered her horse to a nearby sapling. All her anger had disappeared, and she was laughing gaily as she chased the bear cubs through the underbrush. She called to Dave to come help her.

The cubs were yelping in terror, uttering a curious cry, short and sharp, that sounded like a child's urgent call for help. Dave tied his horse and joined in the chase, but the cubs were too elusive in the thick brush.

Dave caught Catherine's arm. "Leave them alone a few minutes," he said. "They'll come back to their mother."

She nodded, panting for breath. Her eyes were flashing gleefully and her face was bright with pleasure.

"I want them, David," she said. "Can't we catch them?"

"We'll try," he said. "They'll come back to the she-bear. They don't know anyplace else to go."

"Poor things," she said. "I feel sorry for them."

Dave led the horses some distance into the woods and tied them there, then he and Catherine hid beside the log. A few minutes later the cubs ambled out of the brush and began nosing about the body of the dead bear. They whined piteously as they paced around the massive body. At Dave's signal he and the Indian girl rushed from concealment and ran for the cubs. Dave caught one by the hind legs in a diving tackle, but the other one got away from Catherine. The captured cub began to cry in terror. Catherine vanished in the brush, racing after the second cub.

The fat little animal in Dave's hands twisted and squirmed, trying to bite him. Before he managed to pin it to the ground, its needle teeth sank into his wrist. He called to Catherine.

Together, after a considerable struggle in which the cub's jaws snapped continuously, they managed to get it into a sack. Dave tied the drawstrings and handed the sack to Catherine.

"There's your pet," he said. "I don't know what you're going to do with him."

"I'll keep him," she said gaily. "I'll have a trained bear."

"Train him not to take your hand off," Dave said ruefully, looking at his bleeding wrist.

She insisted on bandaging it for him with some strips of the linen shirt that he'd left lying on the ground. As she concentrated on the wrapping, her cool slim fingers on his arm and her dark braids swinging against his shoulder, he thought again how pretty she was. She seemed to like him too. He wondered if he could see her again. It would certainly be pleasant to have someone to talk to besides the unfriendly Isaac.

If I give my parole to Brant, he thought, then I can come and go as I please. I could come over here any time I wanted to. I'd like to see her again.

As if she could read his mind, she looked up at him quizzically. "What are you thinking, David?"

He smiled at her. "I was wondering, supposing I had the chance, if I could come over here to visit you."

She bowed her head over his hand. "I would be glad to see you, David," she said softly.

The work of skinning the bear and butchering it took Dave more than an hour. When he and Catherine returned to her father's cabin, Joseph Brant and Dr. Guthrie of the Rangers were already there. Brant told Dave that Isaac was asleep under the effects of an opiate.

"Dochstadter told me what you did, David. I thank you for it. We'll never forget it."

"If I had moved faster, Isaac wouldn't have been hurt at all. I'm sorry about that."

"You saved his life, David. He and I are forever in your debt. Tell me this. Didn't it occur to you that you could have left him there and made your escape? It's springtime now. With your knowledge of the woods and a few hours' start, you could have managed to outrun the Indians we'd send after you."

"I wouldn't have left him."

"Someday I may be able to repay you."

"It's not necessary, sir. I did what anybody would have done."

"Nevertheless, I am grateful. I won't forget. I'll see what

I can do about hurrying your exchange, but you know that's a slow process. You may be here for the duration of the war."

Dave wished he could find the right words to thank Brant, but he stood there silent and uncomfortable.

Brant began to pace the length of the log cabin, talking as he walked. "This accident to Isaac changes some of my plans. I have news that will have some effect on you. This morning I sat in council with the several Mohawk chiefs who are at Niagara. They have finally agreed to take as many Indians as will go with them to settle new lands in Canada, which will ease the long upriver haul with food supplies. General Haldimand has been urging us to move the Indians to Canada ever since Sullivan came through their country."

He paused, and Dave wondered how a migration of Indians could concern him.

"The trouble is that only the Mohawks will go," Brant continued. "We'll try to persuade the others, but I doubt if we will. Now Isaac is hurt. I have to go away to make arrangements for moving the people, so I've had to make new provision for you. You'll work with Captain Millard, at least until Isaac has recovered."

"What about the fields?" Dave asked. "We're ready to put the crops in."

Brant smiled. "So is Captain Millard. You can be of far more help to him. I'll find a Seneca family to take over your work."

While Brant was in the cabin again, talking to Dr. Guthrie, Dave was storing the sacks of bear meat in the springhouse near the barn, against the time when Dochstadter's wife could find time to preserve the meat. As he worked, he thought about his new situation. It would be a relief to get away from Isaac for a while. The constant hostility had been trying for both of them. They had scarcely exchanged a civil word in weeks—even this morning, during the relaxation of the hunt, they had taken no pleasure in each other's company.

Dave hoped he'd like working for Millard. He'd seen the captain at Niagara and had heard much about him. Evidently Millard was one of Colonel Butler's most trusted officers, and Dave knew that Millard was a good farmer—he'd been the overseer at Butlersbury, the Butler estate, in the years just before the war.

At any rate, Dave gave no thought this time to protesting that he should be lodged in the jail at the fort with Corporal Betts and the others. The freedom he enjoyed as Brant's personal prisoner was much too pleasant, he admitted to himself, to be exchanged for a wooden bunk in a stone cellar. His comrades in the prison could never forget that they were captives, living out their dreary days of imprisonment with only the hope of exchange to keep them from despair, while he could do the work that he loved best from dawn to sunset. He could watch the soil put forth its abundance under his skilled hands, and for hours at a time he could lose himself in the thousand pleasures of farming, forgetting that he was a prisoner.

CHAPTER EIGHT

"I don't promise you anything but hard work," Captain Millard said. He had a ready grin that made Dave take to him immediately.

"I'm used to that," Dave said.

"Joseph told me that you can read and cipher and that you're a good farmer. I can use you."

"I'll be glad to work, Captain," Dave told him, "as long as what I do doesn't help your army."

"All my efforts are for the starving Indians," Millard said. "We hope to feed them all through the next winter. None of the food we raise goes to, the garrison and very little of it to the Rangers. So it's a bargain?"

"Yes, sir."

"All right, let's get to work. There's a shipment of seed for us at the commissary. We'll have to take it across the river."

They were standing on one of the docks at the river front below the fort, where Joseph and Dave had met Millard. Now the captain led the way to the fort and the commissary buildings, walking swiftly in spite of his noticeable limp. He had been wounded by a rifle bullet in the attack on Cherry Valley.

Dave thought he would get along well with Millard. The Ranger captain was a tall, lean man probably less than thirty years old, with a long, angular face, weathered by wind and sun. His dark curly hair was cropped close, in contrast to most of the Ranger officers, who wore theirs long and usually tied with a thong at the neck. Millard was pleasant and soft-spoken, again in contrast to most of the other Rangers, who were hard-bitten woodsmen.

When they reached the commissary office, Dave was happily surprised to find Sam Hawkins, wrapped in a linen apron, behind the counter. Sam was stocking board shelves with Indian trade goods under the supervision of a bespectacled young man dressed in a similar apron. Captain Millard started talking to the other man, whom he called "Mr. Goring," while Sam rushed around the counter to pump Dave's hand.

"What you doing here?" Sam demanded.

"I was going to ask you that," Dave said.

"They asked for somebody that could keep store," Sam said. "I told 'em I could and they sent me here to work. It's better than bein' cooped in that jail all the time."

"Here! Here!" Mr. Goring said in a high-pitched, peevish voice. "You, Hawkins! Get back to work, sir, or I'll clap you back in your cell. You're not supposed to be loafing. Get to it, man."

Sam winked at Dave and reluctantly returned to the shelves. Dave stood aside, waiting for orders from Millard, but he soon had another opportunity to talk with Sam, because Goring assigned Sam to help with the seed. The two young men spent the next half hour carrying sacks of seed from the warehouse to the dock, where Millard had two boats waiting to receive them.

The first question Dave asked was about Betts and the others.

"They ain't in such good health," Sam said, "but none of them is real bad off. Just coughs and colds and such. There ain't been any word about sending us down-river to Quebec. The river's open. They ought to send us soon. What you doin' with that Ranger, Dave? I thought Brant took you off."

Dave explained that Brant was taking most of the Mohawk families to Canada and had put him in Millard's custody.

"I'd rather storekeep than farm," Sam said. "It ain't hard work, and that Goring ain't as bad as he sounds. He's always tellin' me I'm going back to jail, but he don't mean it. He locks me in the warehouse at night, and that's a sight better than the prison. I get plenty to eat and lots of free time. You tried to run off again?"

"Not yet. Brant's son has been watching me all the time. He doesn't like me and I don't like him. We had a fight less than an hour after I got to Brant's house."

"Who won?" Sam asked, grinning.

"Neither," Dave said. "It was never settled. He pulled a knife and started to come for me, but his aunt stopped him. I guess he was fixing to kill me."

Sam whistled. "I'm glad I don't have to put up with Injuns. How does Brant treat you?"

"Fine," Dave said. "From what he's said, I suppose it's because I remind him of my father. He tries to make me feel at home."

"Don't get to like it too much, Dave. You'll forget about wantin' to go home. I wish we could be together.

I wouldn't dare try escapin' alone, but I'd go with you, happen we got the chance."

"We'll get it sometime, don't you worry."

"I'd sure like to see my folks again," Sam said. "They probably gave me up for dead a long time ago."

Millard and Goring followed the young men down to the boats as they carried the last sacks of seed, then Sam was immediately hurried back to the warehouse. Millard engaged as rowers four Rangers who were waiting for a ride across the river to the Ranger barracks. During the journey across the stream, Dave sat beside Millard on the piled sacks of grain, listening to the captain explain Colonel Butler's project to furnish food for the civilian population of Niagara and the Indian villages nearby. With a sweep of his arm Millard indicated the fifteen or twenty farms on the sloping land beyond the Ranger barracks.

"All those farms," he said, "are run by Rangers too old for field service or partially disabled in some way. I'm in charge of what they produce. It's our job to see that they get seed and tools and stock and that the crops are divided fairly among the people who need them. Your General Sullivan, Dave, caused us a lot of trouble."

"I saw some of the villages when we came through from Stanwix," Dave answered.

"I don't blame Sullivan," Millard remarked. "He was following orders. I'll be glad when the war is over. I guess we all will. My father used to say that civil war is man's worst crime. You and I, Dave, ought to be back home in the Mohawk Valley, sowing our crops in peace and living quietly with our neighbors."

"You can go back when the war is over," Dave said.

"You think I can?" Millard asked musingly. "I'll tell you, Dave. We'll never go back. There are many among us who think they will—who think we'll win the war and return to our homes and take up our former life. A few of us know better. We have served with the Indians now since the beginning. We led them against the frontiers, and the people in the settlements won't forget our names. You have lived with Joseph now for some time. Do you think he plans to go back?"

Dave shook his head. "He thinks you might lose the war, Captain."

Millard nodded. "Joseph is a remarkable man in many ways. He has his faults, and sometimes the coating of education and our civilization drops away from him and he's all Indian. But he is a smart man. He thinks we might lose the war, and so we might." Millard continued with a grim smile, "Our army—the British Army, that is—will never understand that all colonials are not blockheads. They have no use for our knowledge of the country and our ability to fight the only kind of war that can possibly succeed. If they knew a little more about America——" Millard broke off his remark with a short laugh. "Never mind that. Where do you come from, Dave?"

"Cherry Valley," Dave said.

A shadow crossed Millard's sunburned face. He touched his leg, as if reminded of his wound. "Were you there when we came down?"

"My mother and brothers and I got away," Dave said. "I watched from the hills. My father was killed."

"By the Indians?" Millard asked.

"I don't know. Maybe it was the Rangers. He was trying to get through to the fort."

"It was a bitter day," Millard said simply. "I fear that it will never be forgotten or forgiven. Do you think, Dave, that your people would ever let us come back to live among them in peace?"

"No, I don't think so."

"That's one of the reasons I'll not go back to Butlersbury. I got this game leg at Cherry Valley."

When they reached the far shore of the river, they loaded the bags of seed into an oxcart with the help of the Rangers who had rowed the boat. Then Millard and Dave went inland from the river to the captain's farm, which was not far from Dochstadter's. The acreage that Millard had cleared since the autumn of 1779 was choice farmland that promised abundant harvests. The fields were separated by neat rail and stone fences. The house was a simple two-room log cabin set on a hillside overlooking the fields. It had a wide veranda shaded by an elm-bark roof; there were neat white curtains framing the front window—a glass window instead of the usual oiled paper—and the cabin itself was shielded from the bitter Canadian winds by a grove of hemlocks that rose high on the hillside above.

There was a pretty young woman standing on the veranda when Millard and Dave came up the trail from the river. She held a small child in her arms. Seeing Millard approach, she put the child, a boy with curly dark hair, on the ground, letting him run to Millard with the awkward steps of a baby who has just learned to walk.

She followed the boy, who was squealing with joy as Millard swung him high in the air.

"My wife, David," Millard said. "My dear, this is David

Harper, who will live with us and work with me for a while. Joseph sent him to us."

She told Dave gravely that he was welcome. As he answered politely, thanking her, he noticed that her hair was black and braided in Indian style, that her face had a touch of the same copper tone that he had noticed in Catherine Dochstadter's features, and that her musical voice was careful with English words, as if she were far more accustomed to using another language. He wasn't sure, but he thought she had Indian blood. Later he learned that she was Belle Montour, a member of the noted Montour family of the Seneca nation, which was descended from French traders who had lived among the Indians in the days when Niagara had been a French stronghold.

Now he thought he understood why Captain Millard, during the crossing of the river, had said so positively that he knew he would not go back to the Mohawk Valley to live after the war. Even Sir William Johnson had not been able to force the valley people to accept his Indian wife.

It was almost time for the evening meal when they arrived at the cabin, and while Mrs. Millard was putting it on the table, the captain and Dave went to the barn to see the stock. Millard had several cows, a yoke of oxen, a team of work horses, as well as two saddle horses, a hog, two sows, and two litters of pigs. Mrs. Millard kept a yardful of chickens.

Leaning on the barnyard fence, Millard told Dave about the work ahead of them. "We'll distribute the seed we brought over the river to the farmers here, according to their acreage. We'll sow our own share, and what's left over we'll give to the Indians up near the falls. I had a letter from Quebec when the river opened this spring, telling me that another shipment of seed is on the way. That will be for the Indians out along the Genesee. You and I will make the trip to deliver it to them. It ought to be here any day now."

Dave was pleased at the prospect of visiting the Indian country without fear of being stoned and beaten. He might even get the chance to escape. His blood raced at the thought.

Evidently his face showed his excitement, and Millard guessed what was going through Dave's mind.

"I plan no particular measures to guard you, Dave," he said quietly. "When we go into the Indian country there will be two Rangers with us. They and I know every inch of the country between the Genesee and Fort Stanwix. I don't think you'd get very far."

Dave didn't answer.

"While you're here on the farm," Millard continued, "I'd like to keep the same rule that Joseph had. No attempts to run off between sunset and dawn. Agreed?"

"Yes, Captain."

"We'll get along, Dave."

"I'm sure we will."

CHAPTER NINE

The days on the Millard farm went by swiftly. From dawn until dusk Dave and the captain were busy in the Millard fields or helping the other farmers—all ex-Rangers—to get their seed into the ground. On the second day they visited the Dochstadter place, and Catherine took Dave into the house. Isaac, weak and feverish, was under the constant attention of Dochstadter's wife.

The young Indian's face was impassive when he looked up at Dave. "My father tells me you saved my life," he whispered. "I thank you, although I do not like to owe such a debt to an enemy."

"You don't owe me anything," Dave said.

"It must be repaid," Isaac said. "That is the Mohawk custom."

"We can let things stand the way they were before," Dave said. "I hope you get well soon."

Dochstadter's wife spoke softly in Seneca at this point, and Isaac nodded.

"She says you must go now. She wants me to go back to sleep."

"Is there anything I can get for you?" Dave asked.

"Nothing. These people will see to my needs."

Catherine was eager to have Dave see the bear cub. She led him out to the barn, where the little black animal was chained to a ring in a foundation log near the horse stalls, much to the distress of the horses, which began to stamp and move about nervously when the cub lunged at its chain.

It sounded its curious yelping cry when it saw Dave and Catherine approaching.

"He's getting used to me, David," the girl said happily. "See how he lets me pet him." She put her hand to the cub's head and was rewarded by a nip of the sharp teeth. She shook her hand in pain and shouted a few angry words in Seneca at the cub.

Dave grinned. "He's getting used to you, all right. Wait until he gets a little bigger. He'll take your fingers off. Have you named him?"

"Not yet," she said, glaring at the cub. "But I have a good name for him." She pronounced a long string of Seneca syllables.

"What does that mean in English?"

"It is hard to change the words. It means something like 'The one who bites the hand that feeds him.'"

"I'd like to learn your language," Dave said. "I was trying to learn Mohawk by listening to Colonel Brant and Isaac. Seneca doesn't sound much different."

"It isn't," she agreed. "Would you like me to teach you Seneca, David?"

"We wouldn't have the chance," Dave answered regretfully. "I can't come here any time I want to."

He was interrupted by Captain Millard, who had come around the corner of the barn, seeking Dave. "I don't see

why you can't, David. I don't tie you up at night or on
Sunday."

"You mean I can come here whenever I'm not working?"

"As long as I have your parole—we'll include Sunday as
well as sunset to dawn—you can go anywhere you please
when our work is done."

"Thank you very much."

Dave was more than ever thankful that he had been
kept out of the Niagara jail. He was pleased with the freedom that Millard gave him, although his parole restricted
the possibilities for escape. Also, Catherine Dochstadter's
bright eyes and pretty face were attractions that made
him think less frequently of Hannah Armstrong. There-
after he visited the Dochstadter house as often as he could
in his free time.

Isaac recovered rapidly from his wounds and within
a week was sitting outside the cabin in the warm evening
hours. He was a silently hostile, somewhat contemptuous
auditor while Dave and Catherine labored at Dave's lessons in the Seneca language. Catherine's mother, who seldom spoke on any occasion, sometimes took a hand in
Dave's lessons, intoning Seneca words and phrases in a
low voice. She repeated them methodically until she was
satisfied with his pronunciation, though she never spoke
a word of English.

Dave took more and more pleasure in Catherine's gay
company and counted those evenings lost when bad
weather or the pressure of work kept him away from
Dochstadter's house. He gradually realized that Isaac's
continued hostility had another source; apparently the
young Mohawk had considered himself first in Catherine's

affections until Dave had arrived. But Dave wasn't overly disturbed by her obvious preference for his company instead of Isaac's. If Isaac wanted to carry on the antagonism because of Catherine, Dave wouldn't back away from trouble.

John Dochstadter, during this time, was away on a scouting expedition into the Mohawk Valley. Dave gathered from what Millard and Brant said that there were small raiding parties going out constantly against the New York and Pennsylvania frontiers but that no major excursions were in sight. The last great effort against the settlements had been Sir John Johnson's great raid of October 1780, when he had left a wide path of destruction in the Schoharie and Mohawk country. Even small raids, however, could bring death and destruction on the outlying settlements. Dave wasn't worried about his family—his uncle's farm was within sight of the Middle Fort in the Schoharie Valley, and the Schoharie militia had developed such a fine scouting network after the war's earlier raids that no small war party could reach the rich farmlands of Schoharie without meeting stiff resistance.

All that a party like Dochstadter's could do these days was to hit and run on the fringes of the populous areas. Millard said it was unlikely that any big raiding parties would be sent until the problem of supplies had been solved. With the destruction of the towns in the Six Nations' country, there were no advanced bases for the raiders, and they had to carry their supplies all the way from Niagara to the settlements.

Several times during his first weeks with the Millards, Dave was sent across the river to the fort on various errands. Each time, whether or not he was directed to go to the commissary, he managed to see Sam Hawkins. Mr. Goring always fussed and fumed at the idea of two prisoners taking such social advantage, but he never intervened directly.

"He ain't such a bad feller," Sam said on one occasion when Goring had stamped out of the store after muttering about the amount of work that Sam should be doing instead of talking. "He wrote a letter to his uncle in Montreal to try to find out about exchange. His uncle is some kind of big merchant there. I don't think it'll do us any good, but he tried, anyway."

"I wouldn't want to hang until we get exchanged," Dave said. "We'd best figure on escaping."

"How we ever goin' to do that, with a thousand soldiers to watch us and three times that many Indians who'd like nothin' better than to lift our hair?"

"We couldn't do it from Niagara," Dave agreed. "We'd have to get away from here. Captain Millard is going to take me into the Indian country, but Rangers are going with us. I wouldn't get far if I tried. But the chance will come, Sam. You be ready when it does. I just hope we can go together."

"I ain't so sure you're as set on goin' as you say you are," Sam remarked shrewdly. "I been hearin' about you and that Injun girl. Folks talk to me all the time, Dave, when they come in here. You ain't forgettin' Hannah, are you?"

Dave flushed. "I haven't forgotten Hannah," he said shortly, although his conscience told him that he'd been thinking about her less and less since he'd started visiting the Dochstadter place. Somehow Catherine, who showed how much she liked him, seemed more real to him now than Hannah.

"I got an idea she's waitin' for you to come back to Stanwix," Sam said. "If I was you, I wouldn't get as friendly with these Tories and Injuns as you seem to be gettin'."

"Don't you worry about me, Sam," Dave said sharply. "I want to get home just as much as you do, maybe more. And when the chance comes, I'll take it."

"Don't flare up, Dave. It's just that I don't want them to be talkin' you into stayin' here any longer than you have to. We don't belong here. They ain't our kind of people."

It was on these trips to Niagara that Dave first learned that he had gained some fame among the Indians. He saw that groups of them eyed him with curiosity whenever they saw him at the water front or inside the palisade, and he now knew enough about them to detect the interest that they tried to mask with impassive faces. It was only after quite a few of Catherine's language lessons in Seneca that he could understand some of what the Indians were saying whenever he walked by. He picked out the words "bear" and "knife" and a remark or two about bravery. He was acutely self-conscious when he realized that one Indian was pointing him out to another as the one who had attacked a raging bear with a knife.

Catherine confirmed Dave's supposition. "I have heard, David," she said, "that several families who have lost sons in the war are going to ask Thayendanegea to give you to them as an adopted son. It's the custom among our people to adopt prisoners who prove themselves worthy. Prisoners of courage and strength are always in demand. Would you be willing?" She smiled as she waited for an answer.

"I have a family of my own back in Schoharie," Dave

said quickly. "Besides, they don't adopt grown men, do they?"

"Age doesn't matter," Catherine said. "Maybe Thayen-danegea will adopt you himself."

Dave glanced at Isaac, who was sitting nearby, wrapped in a blanket against the evening breeze. The young Indian stared back with flashing eyes, leaving no doubt about his feelings on the proposal.

"Do I have any choice in it?" Dave asked.

Isaac interrupted in a cold voice, "Don't worry, Harper. My father would never give his prisoner to another family."

"It would be a good life for you, David," Catherine said swiftly. "You'd be treated as one of us. Many white men have done it and have been much happier than they were in the settlements."

Dave shook his head. "I want to go home as soon as I can."

Catherine sighed. "Well, maybe you will change your mind, David, before the war is over. Just remember that our people would welcome you as one of them."

Maybe Catherine was right—it would be a good life. Dave wondered if Brant was really considering adoption. There was nothing that Dave could do to prevent it, and probably it wouldn't be much different from his present status; maybe he'd have even more freedom. He thought of his mother and the boys. If the war dragged on for several years—and there were no signs that it would not—the boys would be grown and able to take care of their mother. In the meantime, maybe it would be rewarding to become a full member of Brant's family. Isaac wouldn't like it, but if his father wished it, Isaac would have to keep quiet. Maybe he'd get over his hostility. Dave thought not, however, because of Catherine. There was no longer any question about it; Isaac was jealous of her obvious preference for Dave.

At any rate, adoption by Brant wasn't an immediate problem. Dave would face it when it came. Meanwhile, he might get the chance to escape, and then all his problems —Isaac, Catherine, his relationship with Brant—would be solved.

Captain Millard's promised trip to the Indian country came at the same time that Joseph Brant returned from his swift journey to Canada to make the final arrangements for the transfer of Mohawk families to their new homes. The sloop that brought Joseph across the lake from Buck's Island to Niagara also carried the shipment of seed that Millard had been expecting. In a conference on the day of the sloop's arrival, Millard and Joseph agreed to visit the Indian villages along the Genesee together. Orders had come from Governor Haldimand that Joseph was to make all efforts to persuade other Indians to accompany the Mohawks. Brant and Millard agreed that they had a joint project—if Brant's persuasion failed, then Millard was to distribute the seed for this year's crops.

It was nearing the end of May when Captain Millard turned the care of his farm over to his wife, who had two Rangers assigned by Colonel Butler to help her. Dave and Millard went to Niagara, where the grain was transferred from the hold of the sloop to a string of pack horses. The party, consisting of Millard, Brant, Dave, and two Rangers, set out from Niagara for the Genesee River.

At village after village at which they stopped during the first part of the trip, the same procedure was followed.

The Indians called a council to discuss Brant's proposal that they move to Canada with the Mohawks. Some of the villages were inhabited by Senecas, some by Cayugas, and a few by Onondagas, but the councils were all similar in ceremony. Dave was fascinated by them.

He usually sat by invitation between Brant and Millard, facing the ring of sachems, chiefs, and warriors of the village. Most of the villages had council houses, or at least a long house that could be adapted for a council meeting.

Dave was impressed by the ritual of the councils, but to Brant they were only a saddening reminder of the lost glory of the Long House. In the old days, the chief told Dave, speakers in council spent days and sometimes weeks preparing their speeches. They dressed in ceremonial robes and headdresses. They bedecked themselves in their finest jewelry and ornaments. No decision was reached in haste, nor was any bickering or acrimony ever permitted before the council fire.

In the old times, Brant pointed out, when the power of the League of the Iroquois was at its height, the nations acted in concert after council debates had determined the majority opinion. It wasn't that way any longer, the chief said bitterly.

The attitude of all the nations except the Mohawks was typified at the first council meeting of the journey, held at the big Seneca town of Buffalo Creek near the shore of Lake Erie. At Buffalo Creek lived many of the refugees from the devastated Seneca villages in the lake country east and southeast of the Genesee River. These people were in worse circumstances than any Dave had yet seen. Brant explained that they had borne the brunt of Sullivan's destruction; their villages had been burned to the ground, and they had been resettled at Buffalo Creek with no possessions except what they had carried on their backs in the long flight from their homes.

The leader of the Indians at Buffalo Creek was an ancient Seneca sachem named Sayengeraghta, or "Old Smoke." He had been the most powerful leader in the nation for many years—he had been a sachem before Joseph Brant was born. His word was still law to the Senecas. Daniel Millard told Dave that there had always been ill feeling between Joseph and Sayengeraghta. It had been much worse in the early days of the war, when the old man had counseled Seneca war parties against taking the field under Brant's leadership. He disputed Brant's claim to the title, "War Chief of the Six Nations," maintaining that his son-in-law, the Seneca chief John Montour, should lead the Long House in battle. The Senecas could put a thousand warriors in the field, while Brant had only a hundred Mohawks to command.

The council meeting at Buffalo Creek was held during the afternoon of the day that Brant's party arrived at the village. The meeting place was a long house of the traditional pattern. It was a hundred feet long and about twelve feet high, built of great sheets of elm bark lashed to a framework of poles. In a permanent village the council house was used only for ceremonial meetings and for the display of trophies and memorials. This one, however, served double duty as a dwelling for several Seneca families. There were sleeping shelves along the walls, curtained by tanned hides. The space above and below each shelf was used as storage room for personal possessions and household goods.

Dave looked around curiously when he entered the long

house. This was the first one he'd ever been in, although his father had often described them to him. Dave noticed several big fireplaces set in the center of the room along the length of the building. In one of them a crackling fire was burning in spite of the warmth of the day. He supposed it was traditional to keep a fire burning during a council.

There were no chimneys to take the smoke out of the room. Instead it curled upward and was sucked through a vent in the roof. Dave thought wryly that he'd just as soon stay out of a long house on a blustery winter's day when all the fires were burning. The elm-bark walls, he thought, must certainly let the wind sweep across the fireplaces. If a man didn't get cinders in his eyes, he was sure to be choked by smoke.

The leading men of the village filed into the council behind Brant, Dave, and Millard. The last man to enter was Old Smoke himself, wrapped in a scarlet blanket and bearing himself erectly in spite of his advanced years. All the other Indians stepped aside until the old Indian had selected his place before the fire. He wrapped his blanket closely around his body, as if he were cold. While the others took their places, Sayengeraghta stared moodily into the flames. The firelight reflected from his dark, sunken eyes. His cheeks were lined and leathery and seemed to bear a perpetual scowl. At the old man's right hand sat John Montour, who was his son-in-law and the brother of Daniel Millard's wife. He was a bronzed, hawk-faced man wearing a green uniform jacket befitting his rank as captain in the Indian Department.

Dave was surprised to see that all the Indians smoked their own pipes. He had always heard that one pipe was passed around the circle. Brant and Millard were also solemnly puffing on long-stemmed clay pipes. Sayengeraghta accepted the pipe offered him by John Montour, closing his eyes as he puffed. He appeared to be asleep.

One of the warriors left the circle and returned in a few seconds with a pipe for Dave, who was the only man in the assembly not smoking. The bowl was filled with a mixture of crushed leaves of different shades of brown. The Indian who had brought the pipe held a burning twig to the bowl. Dave puffed vigorously, and the smoke went into his lungs. The effect was immediate. He thought his throat and lungs were burning. He was racked by coughing until Captain Millard pounded his back. Tears came to his eyes.

"They mix sumac leaves with their tobacco," Millard whispered. "Take it easy. You'll have to get used to it."

"I thought it was gunpowder," Dave answered when he recovered his voice. He looked up to see the dozen Indians opposite him staring intently at him with solemn faces. By this time he was familiar enough with Indian mannerisms to know that they were highly amused. He looked dubiously at the pipe and grinned at the Indians. The row of impassive copper masks didn't change, but he knew they were pleased to see him take the joke.

The council started when Old Smoke opened his eyes and looked steadily at Joseph Brant for a few seconds. Then he grunted a word or two to John Montour. At this signal a young Indian in a British military jacket of brilliant scarlet cloth rose solemnly to his feet and started to speak. His voice, in spite of his obvious youth and slender frame, was deeply resonant, and he spoke easily and clearly. Dave could understand most of the young man's words. It was a speech of welcome for Brant and Millard, telling of their bravery and skill in war and the high esteem in which the Senecas held them. Then, to his astonishment, Dave heard the young orator telling of the white youth who had killed a she-bear with a hunting knife.

Dave's face reddened, and he stared at the packed clay floor.

"You know what he's saying?" Millard whispered.

Dave nodded.

"Look up at him," Millard said. "Be proud of what you did. They'll think better of you."

The Senecas of Buffalo Creek, the young man said, were glad to welcome at their council fire the stranger who had saved the life of Thayendanegea's son. All the Senecas remembered the white youth's father, he continued, as an honest trader who had lived among them and had never tried to cheat them or rot their innards with cheap whiskey. Even though he was a soldier in the army of the Yankees, the young stranger was freely offered the hospitality of the Long House.

The young Indian continued to speak in warm tones about the guests, and Dave had the definite feeling that he was among friends. Meanwhile, Old Smoke apparently went to sleep again.

Joseph Brant put his hand on David's shoulder. "The story traveled swiftly, David," he said in a low voice. "All the people will know it soon. There is nothing they admire more than courage."

Dave, pleased at Brant's obvious pride in him, turned eagerly and asked, "Who is he?" nodding at the young orator.

"His name is Red Jacket," Brant whispered. "He's not much of a warrior, but he's a great talker."

There was a note of scorn in Brant's voice, and Dave later learned that the Mohawk chief blamed Red Jacket for the precipitate flight of the Indians before Sullivan's army. Many years after the war, when Red Jacket was the brilliant spokesman for his people in their negotiations with the United States, Brant's story of Red Jacket's cowardice in battle was often repeated.

"You'll have to answer him, Dave," Millard said with a smile.

Dave looked at the Ranger in alarm. "I can't talk Seneca."

"Speak English. Most of them understand it."

When Red Jacket sat down, Brant and Millard nudged Dave to his feet. Ill at ease, Dave cleared his throat and searched his mind for an appropriate reply.

"Thank you for welcoming me to your village and your council," he said slowly. "I am glad to be here."

He sat down again, embarrassed at his inability to make a speech. His two sentences seemed so little after Red Jacket's eloquence.

Captain Millard grinned at him. "You should have bragged about killing the bear. They all blow their own horns in council."

After a pause in which pipes were again tamped full of the foul-smelling, bitter-tasting tobacco, the regular business of the council started. Joseph Brant got to his feet. He had never seemed more commanding, more impressive. His keen eyes went around the circle of impassive faces and rested on Old Smoke's wrinkled features. The old Indian opened his eyes, blinked them once, and stared steadily back at Brant. The Mohawk began to speak.

He spoke slowly, emphatically, and his powerful voice reverberated from the walls, so that his last word lingered while he spoke the next. It seemed to Dave that there was a chorus of Joseph Brants all speaking at once. Brant spoke in the Seneca language, and Dave was able to follow some of the speech. From time to time Captain Millard helped by whispering English translations of involved passages in Dave's ear.

Dave had known that a speaker in council was likely to take an hour or so before getting to the point of his remarks, because the Indians loved oratory and would listen contentedly all day to a good talker. He was surprised, however, to hear Brant go on interminably about the history of the Six Nations, starting with the founding of the confederacy by Hiawatha hundreds of years before. Brant sketched in passionate words the power and the glory that had come to the Iroquois in the span of years. Dave thought that Brant was never going to reach the point—the removal of Indian families to Canada.

When he did, however, his voice took on even more power and persuasion. He told eloquently of warriors' families living in security with plenty of food and clothing under the watchful eye of the government in Canada while the warriors were off raiding the rebel border. He told how generous the British would be to their Indian allies when they no longer had to haul supplies for non-combatants up the treacherous St. Lawrence. He told the Senecas that his Mohawks were ready to go and were only waiting for their brothers among the other nations to decide to go with them.

He finished his speech with a glowing prediction that the end of the war would come within a year or two, when the Yankee army would meet its final disaster at the hands of the King's troops. Then the people of the Long House would return to their homelands, rich and powerful again through the King's bounty.

Red Jacket spoke next, giving a ringing account of the triumphal history of the Senecas on the warpath, saying that they had always been the keepers of the western door of the Long House and that they would continue to be. He promised great victories over the rebels by the force of Seneca arms. He said the King owed the continued protection of the long Canadian border to his Indian allies, but made no mention of the proposal to move to Canada, nor did John Montour, who spoke after him. Dave supposed that they were leaving the decision to Old Smoke. The old man, as the highest-ranking sachem, had the honor of speaking last. Other chiefs rose after John Montour, making brief speeches about their people's love for the Seneca homeland.

Finally, after about three hours of talking, Sayengeraghta got up with deliberate care. All the Indians fixed their attention on his lined face, shifted position, and settled themselves as if expecting a lengthy harangue.

Old Smoke's speech was surprisingly brief in comparison with the others. He spoke clearly and slowly, and Dave was able to follow easily most of what he said. The old man used simple words and no rhetoric.

"Brothers," he said in preface, as had all the other speakers. He paused and looked around the assembly.

"Brothers. We have heard how the Senecas have guarded the western door of the Long House since the

time when man was young. We will always do so. This is
our land. We have always owned it. We own it now. We
will always own it.

"Brothers. Listen to me! I am an old man. I was living
in the time of the Frenchmen at Niagara. I was living
when they sent their shamans in black robes among us
to teach us about their gods. We kept our own ways. I saw
the redcoats, led by our old friend Johnson, drive out the
French. We kept our own ways and our own land when
the redcoats came. Now the Bostonians say they will
drive the redcoats out.

"Brothers. Listen to me! While a Seneca warrior still
lives to take the warpath, we will not leave our country.
If we do as my old friend Thayendanegea says we should,
we leave this land to go to Canada until the war is over.

"Brothers. I tell you that if we go to Canada we will
never come back. We will lose this country forever. We
must live on it and fight for it.

"Brothers. I say that we will not go to Canada with the
Mohawks. I have spoken."

Sayengeraghta sat down and closed his eyes. Every Indian except Brant grunted approval. Joseph stared at the
old sachem with his black eyes smoldering, but Old
Smoke was apparently asleep again.

"Now it's my turn," Millard said softly to Dave. "I'll tell
them that if they won't move to Canada we'll give them
seed. Then we'll go on to the next town."

"That's all?" Dave asked in surprise. "Won't Colonel
Brant try to persuade them to change their minds?"

"The old man's word is law," Millard whispered. "They
wouldn't move a mile without his approval."

Millard stood up and announced in fluent Seneca that

he had brought seed for their crops and that it would be distributed among them according to the number of people in each family.

Old Smoke continued to sit with bowed head and closed eyes until Millard finished. Then he got up and left without speaking to Joseph Brant.

Millard and Dave and the two Rangers distributed seed, reloaded the pack horses, and the party left Buffalo Creek in midafternoon.

They moved in silence after they left the village, following a well-beaten path eastward along the creek. Dave could understand Brant's frustration, and he found himself sympathizing with the chief's disappointment. At the same time, however, he knew that the American cause would be served by the stubborn attitude of Old Smoke and the other Senecas. The effectiveness of Fort Niagara would be greatly reduced as long as its commissary had to feed the Indian families.

Joseph Brant finally gave voice to his anger and disappointment. "I should have known he'd be against it because I was for it," Brant exclaimed. "He'd rather see his people starve than take Joseph Brant's advice."

"Maybe we can persuade the people in the other villages," Millard said. "They don't have Old Smoke to think for them."

Brant laughed harshly. "You know as well as I do, Dan, that runners are already on their way to the Genesee. Within two days the old man's word will have reached every Indian between here and the rebel frontier. They'll all refuse to go to Canada."

"I'd forgotten how stubborn he can be," Dan Millard said. "I'm sure he knows your plan is best."

"He's living in the past," Brant said. "He doesn't know the old days are gone. What do we see these days?" he asked bitterly. "The leaders of the Long House come to a council meeting in ragged clothes cast off by the soldiers at Niagara. Most of them haven't had a full meal in months. Notice how many of them show the marks of scurvy—teeth missing and raw flesh.

"They didn't come to this council today to talk about the future of our people. They came with their hands out, hoping that we'd have food and clothing for them. They have to beg tobacco to fill their pipes.

"There wasn't one of them," Brant continued, "who listened to what I had to say and judged it himself. They all let the old man talk for them—good times will return if they just sit here and wait!"

"Maybe it was a mistake for you to come," Millard said. "Colonel Butler has a lot of influence with Old Smoke."

Brant shrugged and looked at Millard with a grim smile. "As soon as Old Smoke heard I had anything to do with it, we'd get the same reaction. He thinks I want to be king of the Six Nations. He supposes that if I could get the people to Canada, where they'd be directly under the government's influence, I would proclaim myself King Joseph the First."

Joseph's prediction that word would go out from Sayengeraghta to the eastern villages seemed to prove true as the days passed. In every village, large or small, a council meeting was called. Joseph made his speech about security and plenty in Canada. The answer was always the same. "Feed us here," the Indians said. "We will not leave our country."

A few isolated families—Tuscaroras, Cayugas, and Onondagas—accepted Brant's proposal and immediately packed their possessions and left for Niagara. The Senecas, however, were adamantly unanimous in their refusal to leave their country and received support from the mass of Onondagas and Cayugas. Therefore, in village after village, the party from Niagara distributed the seed that would give the Indians a fair chance to get through the next winter without starving.

While the journey, in its main purpose, was a sore disappointment to Joseph Brant, it was interesting and exciting to Dave Harper. Brant took advantage of the long hours of traveling to instruct Dave in the customs and history of the Six Nations and to point out many things that Dave might otherwise have neglected to observe. Brant's conversations were more than casually friendly; they were carried on in the same paternal tone that he usually used with Isaac. Dave often wondered as the days went by when Brant would speak to him about adoption. Here in the heart of the Indian country the idea did not seem so strange, nor did the prospect of living through his captivity as an Indian, instead of as a white prisoner.

Dave was treated with friendly respect by the Indians in every town, for the word of his exploit in saving Thayendanegea's son from the bear had spread throughout the Indian country. Small boys gathered around him, staring solemnly at the strange white man who had attacked and killed a raging she-bear. The more daring among them often went through a vivid pantomime of the adventure, hacking and stabbing with wooden knives at an imaginary bear.

The everyday life of the Indians was a source of constant interest to Dave, who found that the facts were considerably different from settlers' conceptions of how their savage neighbors lived.

Instead of seeing the men lazing around while the women worked, Dave observed that all the men and boys who weren't away on the usual spring raids along the frontier were engaged in clearing land, building fences, harrowing ground to ready it for planting, and cutting brush from fields that had lain fallow since the mass flight from Sullivan two years before. The Indians worked long hours in the fields, and their women usually worked with them. Dave learned that, once the heavy work was done, the women took over the cultivating until harvest.

Some of their agricultural methods seemed haphazard to Dave, since the Indians had little of the white man's passion for precision. Dave saw no carefully squared fields with straight fences. Their boundaries tended to follow natural obstacles—clumps of trees, brooks, springs, bogs, ridges, and rock outcroppings decided the shape of a cornfield. They planted vegetables in hills rather than rows, and they worked around stumps and large boulders instead of going to the trouble of removing them.

The social life of the people was also fascinating for Dave, and he had the advantage of frequent explanations of curious events by Brant, Millard, and the two Rangers. Brant responded to Dave's interest by taking him with him into the Indian homes and treating him as a companion rather than as a prisoner.

The Mohawk chief always found time to point out and discuss the scores of daily village activities. Dave observed small boys learning to be warriors under the instruction of the old men; he watched the boys at their violent games, all of which were aimed at producing indefatigable hunters and ferocious fighters. He saw that the girls—even toddlers of four years old—were given daily lessons in tanning, sewing, cooking, and handicrafts. Their teachers were elderly women who exercised both patience and stern discipline in handling their charges.

Brant and Millard, both during the journey and in camp, discussed with Dave the ancient social framework of the confederacy. He learned that there were few crimes among the Iroquois—most of them being punished instantly by complete social ostracism. There was no law-enforcement agency other than the council meeting, in which the leaders of the village decided what might be done to an Indian who had broken the rules of the village. Stealing, lying, and slander were almost unknown.

There was a new social problem among the Iroquois, however, as Dave already knew. He saw plenty of evidence that it was uncontrollable. These Indians would give anything they owned for whiskey and rum. With the coming of the white traders, Brant said, the moral fiber of the confederacy had started slowly to disintegrate, as the alcohol did its work. In a few years, Brant feared, his people would degenerate into hangers-on in the border country. All of them—men, women, and children—would be at the beck and call of any white man with a jug of watered trade whiskey.

"You have seen them in the border towns, David," Brant said sadly one night when they were talking around a forest campfire. "You know there are Mohawks and Oneidas who live in squalor in the settlements. They'll sell anything they own, including themselves, for a cup of rum."

"Yes, sir," Dave answered. "And our people sometimes treat them like dogs."

"It seems to be a disease with us," the big Indian said unhappily. "It will wipe us out in time."

One of the Rangers, a harsh-voiced man named Bowman, who came from Pennsylvania, nodded in agreement. "Down home," he said, "the old folks used to say that the only way to deal with an Injun was to get him drunk enough so he wouldn't know or care if you was cheatin' him."

"If we could get them to Canada," Brant said bitterly, "the government could control the whiskey trade. But Old Smoke tells them no and they listen to him. He won't live to see it, but the white man will wash away the Long House—what's left of it when this war is over—by flooding it with rum."

He paused, looking closely at Dave. "There might be some hope," he said, "if there were more white men like your father, David, to live among us and help us control ourselves. Such men could rise to high places in the councils of our people."

"Would they listen to white men, sir?"

"They would," Brant said quietly, "if the white men were to become Indians by adoption. Such a life would be interesting and rewarding for an intelligent young man."

Dave looked levelly into Brant's friendly, inquiring eyes, but he made no reply.

CHAPTER TEN

The party reached Little Beard's Town on the Genesee without achieving much success for Brant's proposal, although Millard had disposed of almost all the sacks of seed. The planting season was already well along, and in every village the people hastened to sow the corn, bean, squash, pumpkin, and other seeds that were given them, sometimes going directly from the pack train to the fields with their shares.

Little Beard showed no more enthusiasm for moving to Canada than had any other village leader. In council, the fierce-visaged chief harshly predicted that the Senecas would drive the Yankees into the sea. There was no need to move from their country. They had pledged their support to the redcoats, he said, and had given it through the war, from Oriskany in 1777 until this moment. It was time, Little Beard declared, for the redcoats to pay for the Senecas' services. It was their duty to see that the Indians did not starve.

"This is the last stop," Brant said after the council meeting. "We might as well go back to Niagara."

"Not without a couple of days' rest, Joseph," Millard

protested. "We've been two weeks on this trip, and another two days won't matter. My game leg needs the rest."

"Whatever you say, Dan," Brant answered dispiritedly. "There's no need to hurry back."

Dave Harper was pleased with the decision to linger in Little Beard's Town. The life of the Senecas was becoming more interesting every day as he learned more about the background of the activities he saw. He was willing to stay for weeks in the free, casual atmosphere of the village, where he was allowed to wander at will. He was no longer conscious of being under the observation of curious Indians. Sometimes he found villagers who were willing to talk to him, and then he'd spend a pleasant hour practicing his Seneca and learning more of the Indians' lore.

Once during the first day, when he was wandering in the fields among the Indians who were sowing the new seed, he found himself at the edge of the forest. He realized that he could vanish from sight in an instant. He knew the trail from Little Beard's Town to Stanwix, and this time he could probably outdistance the pursuit. It would be a long hard run, but he was confident that he could make it. He was deterred, however, by the stirrings of a new emotion that he forced himself to recognize. He no longer felt the driving urge to get back to his own country; under Brant's influence, he was becoming deeply interested in the affairs of the Six Nations and wanted to learn as much as he could. Besides, there was Catherine Dochstadter. He'd been away almost two weeks and he found himself missing her. He hadn't realized how much her gaiety and warmth had come to mean to him. He was eager to get back to Niagara and to tell her about all he'd seen and heard on this trip.

Dave spent the late afternoon in the company of Bowman and the other Ranger, Sergeant Petry, stretched out
on a hillside in the warm sun, watching the villagers work.

In the glare of the setting sun they went for a swim in
the Genesee River. The two Rangers were in a relaxed and
cheerful mood for a change. Usually Bowman was a
morose, silent man who kept his thoughts to himself. Captain Millard had told Dave that Bowman had left his wife
and two sons in Pennsylvania, where they lived with her
family, all active rebels. He brooded about the prospect
that he would never see his boys again.

Petry was serious and plodding, a man without imagination who had joined the Rangers when they were organ-
ized in 1778. His wife had died during their flight from
the Mohawk Valley to Canada early in the war. He hated
all rebels and would have had nothing to do with Dave
if Daniel Millard had not sponsored the young man. Petry
was devoted to Captain Millard.

Lying on the riverbank after their swim, the Rangers
talked about their past lives and about the future. They
knew that they would never return to their old homes—
Petry to the Mohawk Valley and Bowman to Pennsylvania. They had chosen a cause that was now doomed to
defeat or, at best, a stalemate. They had to make new
homes in a strange land, where they would struggle for a
fresh start in the middle years of their lives. Underlying
their casual, languorous talk about what the coming years
in Canada would bring was a note of sadness. Neither of
them had a family to comfort him.

Dave was thinking of Catherine as he listened to them.
He might be spending years in this country, and he admitted to himself that he would like the life. What better

step could he take than to cast his way with Catherine's? He could return to Cherry Valley after the war to take up the land his father had left, and Catherine could go with him. He knew that his mother would welcome her. It seemed so much more practical and reasonable to accept this alternative, living out his captivity in freedom and happiness, than to think endlessly about escaping to go back to help fight a war that was already won.

He remembered Brant's words about the Indians' need for leaders. He wouldn't have to go that far. He need not become an Indian just because he married an Indian girl. Captain Millard hadn't. Dochstadter hadn't.

Briefly the thought of Hannah Armstrong came to him. Guiltily he realized that he had not considered her often in the past few weeks. His mind had been filled with Catherine's gaiety and charm. Anyway, he told himself, Hannah had probably forgotten him long since. After all, there had been but a brief friendship between them.

Dave turned his mind back to the present. He'd learned a lot in his months of captivity at Niagara. For one thing, he knew now that the loyalists were not the heartless fiends that his own side declared them to be; they were men who were convinced that they were fighting in a just cause. If he accepted the opportunity of living among them as one of them, he wouldn't have to espouse the cause. He could remain loyal to the United States. He had learned that the Indians, for all their ferocity on the warpath, were human beings with all the emotions of other men and many virtues to offset their savagery. There was much more, he knew, that he could learn to his advantage if he could abandon his status as a prisoner and move among them, at least until the war ended, as Brant's adopted son. Sooner or later Brant would bring up the subject, and Dave wanted to have an answer for him.

The second day of the stopover at Little Beard's Town dawned in a drizzling rain. Brant said at breakfast that they'd be leaving for Niagara the next morning. After the meal Dave volunteered to take the horses out of the village stockade and hobble them in the rich pasturage near the river. This land was several hundred yards from the center of the village. Petry and Bowman were entirely willing to have Dave take care of the horses alone. If he wanted to work in the rain, they'd let him. They sat back contentedly over steaming mugs of tea when Dave left the long house. Brant and Millard were busy with reports.

Dave walked the beaten path to the stockade, thinking that he had better offer Brant his unconditional parole for the duration of his captivity. In that way, he'd lose his role as prisoner and perhaps pave the way for Brant to offer in turn to adopt him. Then there would be no obstacle to his courting Catherine.

He hadn't reached the stockade when he heard an uproar at the eastern end of the village. He looked back. A long file of warriors and Rangers was coming into the town, and he recognized the man in the lead as Lieutenant Dochstadter. Dave realized that the new arrivals must be the war party that Dochstadter had taken into the Mohawk Valley to harass the people of the German Flats during their spring planting.

He watched the villagers streaming out of their houses to meet the newcomers. Dogs and children raced ahead. Then his eye caught a glimpse of a figure cowering among the Indians as the dogs and children lifted an outlandish clamor. He saw red hair flashing. His heart jumped. He lost sight of the figure in the mob, but there was only one person with hair that color—Hannah Armstrong. He ran toward the melee. Knowing the savagery of the villagers in their treatment of new prisoners, he raced to the edge of the crowd and began to push his way through. The women and children moved aside, but he was faced with a line of painted warriors who guarded two prisoners —one a middle-aged man with bowed shoulders; the other, Hannah. Her hair was matted and snarled, her face was torn and bloody from the slashing of branches and brambles, and her clothing was in tatters.

"Hannah!" Dave cried. "Hannah Armstrong!"

She looked about her in amazement. Her eyes passed quickly over Dave, who was struggling to get through the line of guards, then came back to him. She stared at him in wonder. Then she held her arms out to him beseechingly. He fought fiercely to get through the massed guards, but they pushed him back. A strong hand grabbed his shoulder and twisted him around.

"What's going on here?" John Dochstadter's voice was furious. "You fool! You want to get yourself killed?" He recognized Dave, and surprise blended with the anger on his face. "What is this, Harper? What are you doing here?"

Dave didn't answer the last question. He pointed toward Hannah. "I know her, sir. Let me through to her!" He poured out a flood of words about his long friendship with Hannah at Fort Stanwix. Dochstadter listened with a growing smile. He nodded when Dave paused. "Go ahead to your young woman, Harper. She's had a rough time. She needs some comfort."

He spoke a few swift words in Seneca to the Indians, who opened their ranks to let Dave through. Hannah stumbled to him, and he held her in his arms. She started to cry. Dave tried to soothe her, but she continued to sob and tremble. Before she quieted, resting against his shoulder, Brant and Millard had arrived and were watching Dave and the girl curiously. Dochstadter joined them and began an animated conversation.

Holding Hannah gently and speaking softly to her, Dave felt as if he were being raised from a dream and berated himself for having forgotten her, even briefly. Suddenly he knew that he belonged to his own people and his own country, to Hannah and his family and to Cherry Valley. He knew now that all the bright expectations that he had been fashioning in his mind would never have come true. He would not be happy at Niagara, no matter how long he stayed; it would have been a mistake to marry Catherine, lovely as she was; and he would feel like a deserter every time he faced Sam Hawkins' accusing glance.

The uproar of the villagers subsided quickly when the middle-aged prisoner was taken away by a group of warriors. Some other Indians of the war party had wandered off, but the dozen Rangers were sprawled on the ground near Dave and Hannah. They were watching with idle curiosity a tall, skinny Indian who was glaring at Dave and Hannah. From the corner of his eye Dave saw the warrior's fierce face with its rain-streaked war paint.

"Who is he?" Dave whispered to Hannah.

He felt a shudder run through her body when she looked at the tall Indian. "He's the one who caught me," she answered. "The officer said I belong to him. Dave, what will happen? What will they do with me?"

"You'll be all right," Dave said quietly, wishing he were as certain of that as he tried to sound. He knew how difficult it would be to get her away from the Indian if he wanted to keep her. The angry attitude of her captor left little doubt of that.

"How did they get you?" Dave asked.

She stood away from him, almost recovered from her brief hysteria, and tried to arrange her clothing and hair more neatly. Her voice was steady when she started to talk. "I left the fort one afternoon to pick strawberries in the old garden near Wood Creek. Remember it?"

He nodded, frowning. "Why did you do that? Strawberries aren't ripe yet."

"I know that now, but a soldier told me they were. Maybe he was joking. Anyway, my mother wanted to make pies to sell in the store, so I went for the berries. We never thought there'd be Indians that close to the fort. I stayed in sight of the palisade for a long time, but I couldn't find any strawberries, so I moved along. Before I knew it, I was a few feet from the woods, and he jumped out and grabbed me. I didn't even get a chance to scream. The rest of them were waiting a couple of miles away. The officer was angry at him for taking a chance like that, and they hurried away from there. I had to run for hours. Dave, it was terrible!"

She started to cry, and again Dave tried to soothe her. With an angry grunt the skinny Indian leaped forward and grabbed Hannah's arm. Dave shoved the Indian away, and the warrior's hand went to the tomahawk in his belt. He unleashed a torrent of harsh Seneca, pulling the tomahawk free.

"Let him have her, young feller," one of the nearby Rangers said laconically. Not a man of them had moved.

"Won't do her nor you a mite of good if you're layin' there with a split head. That Injun means business."

The Indian twisted Hannah's arm and started to lead her away. She called desperately to Dave.

"Go with him, Hannah!" he cried. "I'll do something. Don't worry."

Dave hurried to Brant and Millard, who were still talking to Dochstadter some distance away. He started talking rapidly, but Brant held up his hand to quiet him, smiling easily.

"Lieutenant Dochstadter has told me the story, David," Brant said. "The Indian is a Cayuga named Tall Pine, who has lived here in Little Beard's Town for the last two years. He has already told John he wants to adopt her to take the place of his daughter who died during the retreat from Sullivan's army."

"Can you do anything, sir?" Dave asked. "She means a lot to me."

Brant looked at him searchingly. "I can see she does, David. Who is she?"

Swiftly, in a few sentences, Dave told Hannah's story.

Brant nodded. "Maybe I can do something for her, David. I'll do my best, but don't count on anything. I have known Tall Pine for years, and I can talk to him, at least. Ordinarily it's fairly easy to buy a prisoner, but he has already decided to adopt her. That makes it difficult."

Millard touched Dave on the shoulder. "Joseph's word carries weight, Dave. If he doesn't succeed, however, Colonel Butler will make every effort to get her to Niagara. He and Colonel Johnson seldom permit the Indians to keep women prisoners."

"One way or another, we can probably get her away

from him, David," Brant said quietly. "I will try." He paused briefly. "I have been watching your mind and heart at work, David. You were on the point of accepting our way of life, weren't you?"

"Yes, sir," Dave admitted. "I was."

"And now that this young lady has arrived among us you think that you were about to make a great mistake. Is that true?"

"It's true. How did you know?"

"I watched your face when you were comforting her. I can see it now in your eyes. I hear it in your voice." He smiled briefly. "I must say I am sorry that Dochstadter's party brought her here."

"I'm not, sir. Now I *know* I belong with my own people."

"All right, David. I'll see what I can do with Tall Pine."

Brant's oratory or his purse—Dave never discovered which it was—finally persuaded the Cayuga to give up his prisoner. The Mohawk chief came to the long house late in the afternoon with Hannah at his side. She had been given new clothes—a doeskin skirt and a linen short gown—and her hair was combed and shining. She smiled at Dave, looking radiant in spite of the bruises and scratches that marked her face. Dave took her hand and held it tightly.

Brant looked at them impassively, only his dark eyes showing regret. "Here's your young lady, David," he said quietly. "She'll go to Niagara with us."

CHAPTER Eleven

The trip back to Niagara was a pleasant, leisurely journey for the others, but to Hannah and Dave it was exciting as they discovered each other again. The Rangers left Dave and Hannah to themselves during each day's march, but in camp at night Petry and Bowman vied with each other to look to Hannah's comfort. They refused to let her do anything for herself, although she offered to cook and tend the camp. They shouldered Dave out of the way good-humoredly; after all, they said, he had the pleasure of her company all day long.

Dave didn't resent their attentions to her; he was content to sit by the fire, keeping his eyes upon her. He admired anew her slender loveliness, heightened when the fire threw dancing shadows across her face and body, and the courage she had shown during her captivity.

She had been badly frightened when Tall Pine dragged her away for adoption, but since her rescue by Brant she had adapted quickly to the new situation. Dave could see that both Brant and Millard were impressed by her ability to conceal the distress she must feel, and it pleased him that they approved of her. Because of the failure of Brant's plan to relocate the Indians in Canada, the nightly camps on the way back to Niagara might have been cheerless and dull. Instead, they were brightened by Hannah's presence.

During the daily marches Dave took pleasure in her close company, particularly when she spoke of how often she had thought of him and worried about him in the months following his capture. He realized the enduring quality of her devotion; she would make a man a wonderful wife, especially a man who intended to build a home on the frontier, where courage and spirit and endurance were needed above all other qualities. He thanked the good fortune that had brought her to him again.

Millard and Brant were amused to see the stolid Sergeant Petry, who had always classed rebels with rattlesnakes and other venomous creatures, so taken by a pretty young rebel that he whistled merrily as he worked to make her comfortable.

Hannah had the choice food at every meal and the best place at the campfire; she slept each night on a bed of spruce tips that kept her high above the rough ground; she was likely to awake in the morning with two extra blankets covering her while Bowman and Petry shivered in the chill dawn.

Dave and Hannah talked about a thousand things during the long days. He told her of all his adventures since the day in March when Brant had captured the woodcutting detail. He spoke of Brant and his family, of the work he did for Captain Millard, and of his gradual realization that all Tories were not the heartless scoundrels they were said to be.

He told her about Cherry Valley nestled in the wooded hills, and about the rolling stretch of land in the valley bottom that he would farm if he ever got back there.

She, in turn, told him what had happened at Stanwix since he'd been captured—most of it routine garrison life. She spoke of changes in garrison personnel, her mother's store, and told him what she knew of the progress of the war. A British general named Cornwallis was chasing General Greene down south, or maybe it was the other way around. She wasn't sure.

They were both concerned about her future at Niagara, although Dave assured her she would be safe in Brant's custody.

They agreed that the hand of Providence had been concerned in their meeting at Little Beard's Town. If Dave had not been there, she would have lived among the Indians until the end of the war, and they might never have seen each other again. As they approached Niagara, where they might be separated again, Dave wanted to tell her his old dream of taking her with him when he finally went home to Cherry Valley, but he couldn't find the words.

He was afraid she would refuse him. Why should she pick a frontier farmer who had nothing to offer but a life of hard work on the edge of the wilderness? Cherry Valley wouldn't always be the tip of the frontier, but he knew she was used to finer things than a one-room log cabin and the arduous dawn-to-dusk labor of a farmer's wife.

When they reached the plain before Niagara, however, with the distant fort dancing hazily in the shimmering sunlight, he knew that he had to speak. Before he could summon the courage, Brant called Dave and Hannah to his side.

"We must decide what to do with you, now that you're

here," Brant told Hannah. "It will have to be one of two things. You can live with an officer's family here at the fort, doing housework and sewing and such chores. You would be well treated. There are several women brought in by raiding parties who do such work.

"The other alternative," he continued, "is the one that I would favor. My sister is about to leave for Montreal. You can go with her and stay with her there until you are exchanged. She is the widow of Sir William Johnson, and her influence might help to send you through the rebel lines."

Hannah looked puzzled. "I don't know," she said. "I'm your prisoner. You're the one to decide."

Brant nodded, smiling. "I think it best that you go with Miss Molly to Montreal. Your exchange would certainly go through much quicker if she intercedes for you with General Haldimand. You'd be sent to Albany in a matter of days if you're on the spot when an exchange agreement comes through. If you stay here, it might be as long as two years before the people in Quebec get around to including you in an exchange list of noncombatants."

Hannah nodded. "When will I go to Montreal?"

"In a day or two," Brant said. "Molly is waiting for me to return before she leaves. I know David would prefer to have you stay at Niagara, but he'll agree that we should do what's best for you."

"Yes," Dave said hastily, although his spirits had plummeted with Brant's suggestion. "She'll be much better off at Montreal with Miss Molly."

"All right, then," Brant said. "You two say good-by to each other here, because I'm not going to the fort. I'm going cross-country to my house, and the young lady will go with me, David."

He left them there while he went to speak briefly to Millard. Dave took Hannah's hands in his.

"I guess we won't see each other again," he said quietly, looking at the ground. "I'm sorry it has to be this way, but you'll like Miss Molly. She's been fine to me."

"After the war, Dave——"

"The war may last for years," he interrupted swiftly as he found at last the courage to tell her what was in his heart. "I'll probably have to stay here until the end, and you'll be back with your mother at Fort Stanwix or maybe someplace else. I'll come to find you. Will you be waiting, Hannah?"

"Oh, Dave! I'll wait, no matter how many years it may take."

"I'll come to you, wherever you are."

"I know you will! If I'm not at Stanwix, you'll have word where to find me."

Brant was ready to go. He motioned to Hannah to join him. There were tears in her eyes, and her lips trembled as she said unhappily, "Good-by, Dave. Good-by."

He threw his shyness aside and took her in his arms, not caring that Brant and Millard and the two Rangers were watching. He kissed her roughly, feeling the tears on her face wetting his own.

Brant said a few words to Millard, nodding toward Dave and smiling sadly.

Dave kissed Hannah again, gently this time. He let her go. She stood there for a few seconds, looking into his eyes. "Don't forget me, Dave. I'll be waiting."

"No matter how long it takes, I'll come," he answered.

"It may be a lot sooner than we think. You'd better go now, Hannah."

She turned and walked toward Brant. She didn't look back as they took a trail that went west to the river. Dave watched her go. Her red hair was shining in the sun. It was the last thing he saw when she and Brant crossed a rise and passed from sight.

Sergeant Petry put his hand gently on Dave's shoulder. "Don't take it hard, young feller. All wars has got to end sometime. You'll be seeing her."

CHAPTER TWELVE

Through the long, hot summer days Dave and Millard worked side by side in the fields. It was rewarding to see the corn grow tall and green day by day; to see buckwheat and oats rippling in the breezes that flowed in from Lake Ontario; to see squash, beans, cucumbers, and pumpkins ripening in the summer sun. But the thought of Hannah waiting for him was always in Dave's mind as he followed the cultivator and the plodding oxen that pulled it through a sweltering day in the cornfields. He was often tempted to take any chance, no matter how desperate, to escape his captivity, but he had the good sense to realize that the opportunity, when it presented itself, must be a good one. He had learned too much about the Indians and Rangers and their skill in woodsrunning to risk anything that didn't promise the certainty of reaching Stanwix.

Sam Hawkins was just as eager as Dave was to get away, but he confessed to little hope of doing so.

"Goring never lets me get away from the fort," he complained to Dave in a whispered conversation during one of Dave's trips to the commissary. "If I was out in the open all the time like you, Dave, I'd be long gone. They wouldn't see me for dust!"

"It's not as easy as that," Dave said. "A man's got to have a good running start or they'll catch him. The time is going to come, Sam. You wait and see. Some way for us to go together will turn up. I know it will."

"I guess you're not thinkin' so much any more about takin' on Indian ways and such, are you, Dave?"

"Did you think I was going to, Sam?"

"I was worried. You'd come in here talkin' about what a fine feller Brant is, and Captain Millard, and that Injun girl. You had me scared, until you come back from the Injun country with Hannah. Ever since then, you've had that faraway look in your eyes, like you were tracin' every step between here and Stanwix."

"I hope Hannah's back there, Sam. There hasn't been any word from Miss Molly."

"Don't you worry about that, Dave. I had my doubts about Brant in the beginnin'. I thought he was just a fancy-talkin' Injun. But he's done a lot for you—everything he said he would. His sister will see that Hannah goes through on exchange. I wish somebody would do the same for us. I want to go home, Dave!"

"They haven't sent Betts and the rest of 'em down the river, have they?"

"Not yet. I see 'em on work details around the fort. They all look pretty good. Maybe the exchange will come this summer."

"I wouldn't bet on it," Dave said.

Sam shook his head. "I ain't. I just wish Goring would send me out on one of these here trips like you go on. Then we could get together and make tracks."

"I'll manage to get over here if I think there's a chance. Meantime, Sam, all we can do is wait."

During the weeks of the summer Dave restrained his impatience by giving rein to his old enthusiasm for working the land. He was pleased that Millard considered him a good farmer, and he and the captain shared the satisfaction of a job well done. Often in the evening, when the day's labor was done and the stock turned out to graze, they stood together by the barnyard fence, looking across the rolling country marked with brownish-gray fences and green fields, surveying their work and talking quietly of what they might do tomorrow.

In the distance the wooded hills faded into the haze of dusk. Mrs. Millard would come down from the house with mugs of buttermilk chilled in the springhouse. As they stood and sipped the cooling drinks, the lake breezes were soft against their faces. Dave, feeling the drowsiness of the evening steal over him, would be in these moments more at peace with himself than he had been since he'd seen Hannah. Escape was something to think about tomorrow.

Although the work was long and wearying, there was time for other things. There were his visits to the fort, where he could usually manage a few minutes' talk with Sam Hawkins; there were trips to Buffalo Creek and other nearby Indian villages to deliver early crops of beans and other vegetables to the hard-pressed Indian families, and there was always the chance to visit with the Dochstadters for an hour or so in the evenings.

Since Hannah's capture, Catherine's obvious affection for him had become a problem that Dave couldn't seem to face. She was with him constantly during his visits, always vivacious and entertaining. He felt guilty but never mentioned Hannah to her, and he wondered if her father had told her about the red-haired girl. It seemed likely that he had, but she never mentioned it. Dave was often on the point of telling her but kept putting it off. She appeared content just to be with him, and avoided any serious discussions; so Dave didn't know how to tell her there was no chance for anything more than friendship between them.

Isaac knew about Hannah, however, and his attitude toward Dave underwent a gradual change. He had long since recovered from his wounds and was living alone in Brant's house across the river while Brant was in Canada with his Mohawks most of the time during the summer. Isaac, too, came often to Dochstadter's after the evening meal, and it was during one of these trips that he demonstrated his change of feeling.

After dark one evening Dave said his farewells to Catherine and her mother and was about to return to the Millard farm. Isaac said he'd walk a way with Dave. Surprised at the overture, Dave told him to come along.

They were out of hearing of the Dochstadter house when Isaac spoke. "You've had no news of the red-haired girl, have you?"

"Not yet," Dave said.

"My father should be back soon. Maybe he will have word."

"I hope he does," Dave said.

"We have been enemies," Isaac said suddenly. "You know why, don't you, Harper?"

"I think I do," Dave said. "I'm sorry about it. Being here is none of my doing."

"I was angry because my father took such an interest in a rebel, even if your father was his old friend. He intended to treat you like a son and wanted me to treat you like a brother. To me you were an enemy. You still are, Harper."

"I know how you feel," Dave said.

"Then you saved my life when the bear attacked me. I am very grateful for that and have not forgotten it."

Dave didn't answer, and Isaac continued, "Things might have been different after you killed the bear, but then Catherine came between us."

"I know that too," Dave answered.

"I realize now that you do not love her, even though she thinks she loves you. She would never be happy with you, Harper. You could never live among us and be content. You must go home to your red-haired girl and your own people."

"That's right," Dave said. "I have never intentionally let Catherine believe that I meant to stay here."

"Are you going to tell her that you're going home?"

"I will when the time comes. I haven't said anything because I thought it would make her unhappy."

"I have thought that was in your mind. Now that you have told me, we need not be always bitter toward each other. We can be friendly enemies at least, can we not?"

"More friends than enemies, I hope," Dave said, smiling.

"It will please my father to have it so," Isaac answered. "Have you told him you will not stay with us? I am sure he would adopt you according to our custom if he thought you were willing."

"He knows," Dave said slowly. "He understood how it

is with me and Hannah during our return from Little Beard's Town."

They walked in silence a way, then Isaac laughed softly. Dave looked at him questioningly. He could see the Mohawk's white teeth gleaming in the moonlight.

"What is it?" Dave asked.

"You will escape if you get the chance, David?"

Dave hesitated, wondering how far Isaac's new friendliness would go. Finally he said, "Yes, if I can."

Isaac laughed again. "Tell me about it first. I will lead those who chase you on the wrong trail. I want you to go back to your Hannah and leave Catherine to me."

After that evening Catherine was puzzled by the improved relations between Dave and Isaac, but it didn't trouble her long. She continued to devote most of her attention to Dave, an attitude that Isaac now accepted with patience.

Joseph Brant appeared at Niagara only a few times during the summer for brief visits. Once he crossed the river to Millard's with the news that Dave had so anxiously awaited.

"I've had word from Miss Molly, David," he said. "Your young woman will be sent through to Albany in the next exchange of noncombatants. I don't know when that will be, but both sides are always quick to exchange people who can't bear arms. She'll be back home very soon."

"Thank you, sir," Dave answered. "That's the best news I could hear. I appreciate what you've done."

"I seem to have been working against my own interests, David," Brant said quietly. "It is still my wish that you stay with us."

"I know that, sir."

"You've made up your mind, haven't you? There's no question?"

"No, sir. I want to go home."

"All right, David. I cannot force you, and I won't try to persuade you."

Dave thought of Hannah constantly in the weeks that followed, wondering if she were still in Montreal or had already gone through to Albany. Would she be waiting for him at Fort Stanwix? Sometimes he had doubts. The only bonds between them were a few words and a kiss on a forest trail.

Whenever his doubts won the argument over his common sense, he regretted that he had asked her to give her word to wait for him. It would be unfair to hold her to it until she understood what life on a frontier farm would be like. It was true that she had been at Fort Stanwix, far west of the settlements, but that was a military post, having none of the loneliness of the backwoods.

In the meantime, as their friendship grew, Isaac Brant was pressing Dave to return to live with him in the house across the river. He argued that Dave could use a canoe to go back and forth to Millard's, without inconvenience to anyone. Dave held back. There was a question in his mind that would take time to resolve—might not the old hostility between him and Isaac flare again over some minor incident? Further, the trips across the river would add two hours to his long working day.

The frontier was quiet that summer. Small raiding parties—a dozen men at a time—left Niagara and the Indian villages regularly, bound for the settlements in Pennsylvania and New York. They generally failed, however, to do more than burn and pillage a few outlying cabins. Often they were pursued by Continentals and militia and were forced to abandon plunder and supplies in their flight. Casualties were far more frequent among the raiders than they had been in the early days of the war.

"Your rebel friends have learned how to fight this kind of war," Daniel Millard said to Dave one day in September. They stood on the dock near the Ranger barracks, watching a half dozen weary, bedraggled Rangers lift two wounded men from the boats that had carried them across the river. This party had returned from a scouting trip to the Susquehanna country. They had been ambushed by a strong force of militia and had been chased all the way to Tioga Point on the New York-Pennsylvania border.

"They have learned to run for the forts at the first alarm," Dan Millard continued. "Their militia and regular troops are on twenty-four-hour alert. They don't work in their fields any more unless they have armed guards posted, and they keep scouts watching all the trails we have used for years. We haven't been able to damage them severely since Sir John Johnson's raid last fall."

"Maybe the border war will come to an end," Dave said hopefully. He knew from many conversations that Millard had never approved of the Rangers serving with the Indians and had been thankful when he was removed from field duty to supervise the farming project.

Millard shook his head dubiously. "Captain Butler and some of the other officers are talking about a big expedition this fall, when the rebels have their harvest in the barns. I'm afraid the bloodshed is far from over, Dave. I wish it were. I wish that we could all live in peace again."

Late in September, in the middle of corn-cutting on the

loyalist farms on the far side of the river, Captain Millard returned from the fort one day with news important to Dave. They discussed it after the evening meal.

"General Powell has received an order from Quebec regarding prisoners, Dave," Millard began. "I read it at headquarters this afternoon. General Haldimand wants all prisoners now held in the upper posts—that includes Niagara, Detroit, and Michilimackinac—to be sent down to Quebec. They'll be kept in the Dauphin Prison until suitable exchange terms have been arranged for each man."

"That means I'll have to leave here, Captain."

"I don't believe it does, Dave. The order goes on to say that artisans, such as carpenters and blacksmiths, and professional men—doctors, for instance—who are now usefully employed by us may be exempted from the order. Mr. Goring told me that he intends to keep his clerk—what's the young man's name?"

"Sam Hawkins."

"Yes, Hawkins. I asked General Powell if I could keep you, at least until the harvest is finished. He agreed that I could."

That's not so bad, Dave thought. I'll be better off here than in a cold, damp cell during a Canadian winter. And Sam will be here too. We might still get our chance to run off together.

"Will I be sent down to Quebec after the harvest is in?" Dave asked.

"You may be, Dave. I don't know. The river may freeze up early this fall, and if a party doesn't leave for lower Canada before the freeze-up, it's possible that you'll have to stay until spring."

Dave was bitterly disappointed. "That means I'd lose my chance for exchange."

"I don't think it does, Dave. The order says that exchange for the prisoners kept at the Upper Forts will be arranged at the same time it goes through for the prisoners in Quebec. If you're still here, you'll just have a longer journey back to your home."

"How long do you think the exchange arrangements will take?"

Millard shrugged. "Let's face the facts, Dave. They may never be made. Neither side wants to give the other any able-bodied men. All this order from Quebec is intended to do is clear the Upper Posts of prisoners who must be fed with food that's hauled all the way up the river. General Haldimand makes the point that it's much more sensible to take them where the food is rather than hire boatmen to haul it up here."

"So you have decided that I'd better stay here?"

"If Joseph Brant agrees. Remember, you're his prisoner, not mine."

Sam Hawkins reported to Dave that the prisoners had been marched out of the jail at Niagara on the first day of October, put aboard a lake sloop, and sent off to Buck's Island on the first leg of their journey to the prison in Quebec.

"You glad you stayed, Dave?" Sam asked.

"Maybe I am. We may be out here until the end of the war, but we're better off here than spending the winter in prison."

"I think you're right. Mr. Goring told me I was going to stay because he needs me, but he said he'd keep tabs on exchange so I wouldn't lose out."

"That's what Captain Millard promised me."

When harvest time was over, Dave at last returned to the Brant house to live, at Isaac's insistence. He made the daily trip across the river to Millard's in Isaac's canoe, but the farm work required less time and labor. Millard could handle most of it alone.

One morning in the second week of October, Dave walked up the trail from the river to the Millard place and found Mrs. Millard and her little boy Alex packed and ready for a journey. Captain Millard was in the barn. He was wearing buckskin breeches, moccasins, and his green Ranger jacket.

"You all look as if you're going traveling," Dave said after greeting Millard.

"We are," Millard said grimly. "My wife and Alex are going to visit her aunt at Buffalo Creek. You and I are going to drive the stock over to John Secord's place. We'll leave the chickens and pigs here, and John will come over every day to take care of them. You can have yourself a holiday with Isaac for two or three weeks, Dave."

"Where are you going, sir?"

"Remember I told you there'd be a big raid in the fall?" Dave nodded.

"Captain Butler came over to see me last night. We start today. He and I are leading the Rangers and Indians. Major Ross from Buck's Island is in command of the expedition."

"Where are you going, Captain?"

Millard looked at Dave with troubled eyes. "Into the Mohawk Valley," he said shortly.

Dave's heart jumped with sudden fear. Schoharie? Sir John Johnson had covered both the Mohawk and the

Schoharie valleys the year before. Did Ross and Butler intend to take the same route?

Millard seemed to read Dave's mind. "Warrensbush to Johnstown and then along the Mohawk, Dave," he said quietly. "We won't touch Schoharie. That's where your family is, isn't it?"

"Yes. I guess they wouldn't be in much danger, anyway. My uncle's farm is near the Middle Fort."

"No noncombatants will be in danger, Dave, if we can control the Indians."

"I thought you were finished with field service," Dave said.

"I thought I was," Millard answered, turning abruptly to the oxen. "I have to obey orders like anyone else. Let's get to work, Dave."

Dave and Isaac went to Fort Niagara later that day to watch the expedition leave. Several companies of green-coated Rangers climbed into long, clumsy bateaux at the water front, followed by a large detachment of regulars from the British garrison. Everywhere around the fort were the Indians, hundreds of them, silently watching the soldiers embark. It was easy to pick out the warriors who were going with the troops. They were all armed and painted for the warpath. Dave was surprised to see what a motley group they were. A few Senecas, Cayugas, and Onondagas stood disdainfully apart from the rest of the war party. There were a couple of hundred wild-looking Missisaugas from the other side of Lake Ontario—fierce in appearance but useless in battle. With them were some Hurons from Canada, a few renegade Oneidas who had left their own nation to become hangers-on at Niagara, and a dozen ragged-looking Tuscaroras and Delawares.

Isaac laughed when he saw them. "I wonder why Captain Butler bothers to take them," he said. "They'll scatter at the first rebel volley."

A bearded Ranger who was packing a bedroll nearby looked at the young Indian and grunted a disgusted reply. "That's all he can get. Guy Johnson says them Injuns has got to earn their keep around here, so he's sendin' 'em off with us. He ain't givin' us Senecas nor Cayugas. This is all we can have. I'd ruther go without 'em."

When the last bateau had made for the open waters of Lake Ontario, to follow the shore line as far as Oswego, where the troops from Niagara would meet Major Ross and his detachment, the Indian war party straggled away from the fort, headed cross-country to meet them. They were led by a half dozen officers of the Indian service, whose contempt for the fighting qualities of their charges was plain to be seen.

"If my father were here," Isaac said, "he would have taken his Mohawks and some Senecas. All those Missisaugas are good for is burning and killing stock."

"Isn't that what they're going for?" Dave said with controlled bitterness. He was thinking of the settlers in the Mohawk Valley who, a week or so from now, would be watching their homes and barns go up in flames.

Isaac looked sharply at Dave, but he made no comment. Together they stood on the dock, watching the bateaux fade from sight on the blue waters of Ontario.

CHAPTER THIRTEEN

The first day of November dawned cold
and gray, with a raw wind pushing the slate-colored
clouds swiftly across the sky. Rain or maybe sleet was
promised when the wind shifted slowly from southeast to
east and then held steadily in the northeast.

Dave had to remove a thin edge of ice from the water
bucket before sousing his face and shoulders. The river
would soon be closed. Chances were that he was going to
spend the winter at Niagara.

He stood shivering in the chill air while he toweled himself briskly with an old piece of sacking. Looking down
at the river, he could see black patches in the coves and
backwaters. Faintly, above the distant rumble of the falls,
he could hear the squalling of the thousands of ducks and
geese that had come in off the lake the night before when
the wind started to blow. They'd sit on the river until the
weather cleared, unwilling to take flight in the threatening
sky. It would be a good day for shooting.

Isaac Brant came out of the house and stood looking at
Dave with a smile fleeting across his dark face. "You are
thinking as I am, David," he said, laughing softly. "We

should give ourselves a day on the river with the guns. In all my life I have never seen so many ducks."

Dave grinned and nodded agreement. "It sure would be a good day for it. We could kill enough today to last us through the winter and maybe have enough left over to furnish other people."

"Dochstadters could use the extra ones," Isaac said.

"That's right. With Lieutenant Dochstadter away with Captain Butler, they won't have a chance to get any for themselves. There won't be many of these big flights."

"Catherine could come with us," Isaac said. "She could row the boat while we shoot."

"Shall we do it?" Dave asked eagerly. "All the work here is done. What do you say?"

"My father left for the fort before dawn," Isaac said thoughtfully. "He left no orders for us. Let's go, David."

"Good! You get the fowling pieces and I'll pack some food."

"First we'll have breakfast," Isaac said. "I don't like to hunt on an empty stomach."

After they had eaten, they crossed the river in the canoe, passing within gun range of hundreds of ducks and geese without putting them to flight. They climbed the slope to Dochstadter's, where Catherine was just finishing feeding the stock.

She clapped her hands with pleasure when they told her why they'd come. "I'll come right away. Wait until I put heavy clothes on."

When she was ready, dressed in a heavy blanket coat and fur-lined winter leggings, they went down to the river again. They beached the canoe and took John Dochstadter's flat-bottomed duckboat. While Catherine poled the craft through the shallow waters toward the nearest of the bays, Dave and Isaac loaded the fowling pieces. They used bird shot cased and wadded in a paper cartridge and fine French powder for the priming.

The duckboat slid around a point heavily grown with rushes and edged by thick clumps of alders. They were coming into a shallow, sheltered cove. Its surface was literally covered with ducks and geese. There were thousands of them, and their noise made talking impossible. Dave noticed Canada geese, snow geese, and blue geese. Among the ducks were mallards, pintails, whistlers, teal, wood ducks, canvasbacks, redheads, and perhaps a dozen other species.

Dave motioned to Isaac to start the shooting.

Catherine poled the boat out of the rushes into the open water. The wary geese were the first to take alarm. They honked a chorus of warning that drowned all other sound. With a roar of heavy wings beating furiously they began to take the air. Isaac fired into the nearest flight. Dave squeezed the trigger immediately after Isaac's gun boomed. The spreading pattern of shot tumbled a half dozen geese into the water. The second barrels were fired, and more geese fell.

By this time the air was filled with waterfowl. In their rush to get away they collided with each other and crashed through the alder branches. A few seconds later the surface of the cove was clear of all but a dozen or so dead geese. The din made by the flying birds entirely drowned the dull roar of the falls upriver. Dave and Isaac reloaded hastily. They waited in the rushes while the birds flew out over the river in massed flights. Catherine held the boat steady in the rushes with her pole. All three crouched low in the boat.

The geese were gone now; even though few hunters had ever molested them in Canada or their winter homes in the far south, they were wary enough not to return to a place where guns had frightened them. The ducks were another matter; those that had flown out over the river had disturbed hundreds of others in neighboring coves that had joined them in flight. The mixed flocks would come into this cove in great numbers after they'd fought the strength of the wind for a couple of minutes over the open river.

Soon enough the hunters heard the whistling beat of hundreds of distant wings come closer. The ducks began to circle the cove, coming lower with each circuit until they began to set their wings. They came down by scores to land for feeding. Dave lifted himself carefully, looked over the rushes, and estimated that half of the ducks that had been in the cove before the shooting were returning to it. He grinned at Catherine and motioned to indicate that she was to pole them again into the cove.

As soon as the ducks began to take flight, he and Isaac fired again, the four gunshots rolling flatly across the water. This time they killed eight ducks—three canvasbacks, four mallards, and one small wood duck in bright plumage. They picked up the dead ducks and geese, piling them in the bottom of the boat.

"We'll go to the next cove upriver," Dave said, turning to Catherine. "I'll do the rowing."

She was holding the wood duck and stroking its delicately tinted feathers. "Don't shoot any more like this one," she said softly.

Isaac grunted and answered matter-of-factly in Mohawk, "It was an accident. He got in the way. We don't want that kind. They are too small and the breast meat is too thin."

She looked at him scornfully and answered him in his own language. "You are a fool. You don't know what I'm talking about."

"We cannot keep from killing them," he said doggedly. "They fly with the rest. If they go before the gun, they get killed."

"I know what you mean," Dave told her. "It seems a shame when they are so pretty."

She put the wood duck down gently. "We must have food for the winter, but not these lovely ones, David. Give them all to Isaac. They are only meat to him."

Isaac muttered something in his own language to the effect that men who took women along on a hunting trip deserved no better than to listen to nonsense.

Dave smiled and winked at Catherine. She flashed white teeth in an answering smile, holding his eyes fondly with her gaze. They looked at each other for a few seconds, until Dave turned away. He knew that he should have talked to her about Hannah and his determination to go home long before this, but he had kept putting it off, as he had once postponed talking to Hannah until it was too late. He owed Catherine that much—she probably thought he was gradually being persuaded again to accept a future among her people. He must not put it off any longer.

During the morning they went from one cove to another, shooting until the barrels of the guns were too hot to touch. The boat was so heavily laden with ducks and geese that the occupants couldn't move. Finally they put in to shore near a grove of oak trees on the Canadian side of the river.

"You two build a fire," Isaac said. "Make it a big one and let it burn down to coals. I will go shoot some squirrels or rabbits for our meal. They will add to the food that David brought."

"All these ducks," Catherine said, "and you must shoot squirrels?"

Isaac glared at her in exaggerated scorn. "A duck must hang for a week before it's fit to eat. What has your mother taught you all these years? I pity the man who gets you for a husband."

She started to answer angrily, but he stalked away through the oak trees without listening. Dave was laughing at them.

"My husband, whoever he may be, is no concern of Isaac Brant," she said, turning to Dave. "When the war is won, maybe my father will take us to Cherry Valley. The King will give him land anywhere he wants to live. Would you be happy to have us live near you, David?"

He didn't answer, and she looked inquiringly at him. She was the first to speak. Her voice was low and revealed no emotion. "You would be ashamed of us, David? In Cherry Valley you would not be a friend of a person who is half Indian?"

"That's not it at all," he said quickly. He took her hands in his, holding them gently and looking into her eyes. There were half-formed tears on her lashes. "You know I'll always be your friend, Catherine, wherever we may be. I wasn't thinking anything like you said."

"What were you thinking?"

"I didn't want to tell you again that you are wrong.

Your people are not going to win the war. I know it's hard for you to believe it, but your army has already lost. We have fought almost five years for our independence, and we will never give it up now. The King has lost the colonies, Catherine. If he gives your father and the other officers out here any land, it will be in Canada."

"My father promised," she said, staring at the ground. "Years ago he said we would live in the Mohawk Valley after the war."

"Would he go to live among his enemies?" Dave asked quietly. "Would they give him back his land? Would they let him live in peace? It isn't easy for me to say this, Catherine, but I knew the name Dochstadter before I came to Niagara. Your father has led the Indians in a dozen raids on the settlements and has been in a dozen more. The people on my side have suffered in these five years of war. They won't ever hold out their hands to men who have the name Butler or Johnson or Brant or Caldwell or McDonnel or Dochstadter."

"How about you, David?" she asked, keeping her eyes to the ground. "Do you feel the same way?"

"No, I don't. I used to, before I came here. I've learned a lot since I've been here. Your people, both Tory and Indian, think your side of the war is right. I don't. But I know now that your father is not a murderer of women and children, and I know that Joseph Brant isn't either. But the people of the Mohawk Valley will never believe anything else of them. Too many people have been killed and scalped and too many homes burned to let them ever forget the raids or the men who led them."

She turned away from him, and when she spoke her voice was so low that he had to move close to her to hear what she said. "I guess I have known for a long time that what you say is true. I make believe that it is not. That's why I talk of going to the Mohawk Valley. But it doesn't seem right that we can't go to live where we want to! I know that my father dreams that he will go back to his home—maybe he still thinks we'll win the war. I have shared his dream because he is my father."

"He must know the British will quit sometime."

"Maybe he does. There is one thing that makes me think so. I have watched him at night, when he thought my mother and I were sleeping. He goes to the doorway and stands looking eastward to where the moon is rising, and I know he is thinking of the old days. He smiles, and sometimes he whispers to himself. Then he is back among his friends before the war—your people, David, who fight against us now. But sooner or later his face changes and becomes sad, and he stops looking eastward. Maybe then he is thinking that he will never return."

"I think it's best that you face it now," Dave said, putting his hands gently on her shoulders. He realized that this was his opportunity. He cast about in his mind for the words to tell her about Hannah Armstrong.

"I think my mother knows," she said quietly. "She is an Indian, so she is glad that we will not go. I remember that when Belle Montour married Captain Millard, my mother said that he would live with us for the rest of his life. But I know that my mother is sorry for my father because his dream will not come true."

"All the people here at Niagara talk sometimes of going back," Dave said, "but I think most of them know they never will."

"You, David?" she asked tremulously. "Are you sure you want to have that farm?"

He spoke firmly, without hesitation, thinking of Hannah as he did so. "More sure than ever, Catherine. I'll go home as soon as I can."

She turned to face him. She was within the circle of his arms. Her face was lifted toward his, and her eyes were shining. "David," she whispered hesitantly, "why don't you stay with us? We are all your friends. We want you to stay."

"I couldn't stay here, Catherine. I don't belong here."

"I know what it is. It's that red-haired girl my father told me about. You've never mentioned her, but I know when you are thinking of her. Does she live in Cherry Valley, David?"

He shook his head, looking into her tear-filled eyes. "She doesn't live there, but I think she will after the war. I hope she will."

"Do you want to marry her when you go home?"

"Yes, Catherine, I do."

"I guess I knew it all along. I knew it as soon as my father told me about her, but I hoped you would change your mind." She looked at him briefly. "Is there no hope that you will stay with us?"

"None, Catherine. No longer than I have to."

"Why must you go?" she asked with sudden flaring emotion. "I would make you a better wife than the red-haired girl! Can she cook? Can she sew? Can she tan leather? Can she farm your land while you are hunting? I can do all these things, David, and I love you more than she does!"

"Catherine," he said softly, "you tell me your father

looks eastward and dreams when the moon is bright. So do I. I can't help it. Though I'm fond of you, I belong with Hannah and my own people. We have a new country, and we are proud of it. I must be a part of it."

Her dark eyes held his. She was crying and her lips were trembling. He bent his head to hers and kissed her.

"Will you ever come back, David?" she whispered against his shoulder.

"I would like to come here again," he said gently. "I'd like to see you all again. I don't know if I will."

She sighed despondently, and he knew how deeply he had hurt her. He was sorry that he had been forced to bring unhappiness to her when she had been so kind to him through these months. Nevertheless, he was thankful that he had finally told her the truth. Now, if he succeeded in escaping, he need have no qualms of conscience about deceiving her.

They were silent for a few moments. She was looking at the ground. Then she shyly turned her face to his. "David, our people do not kiss. I have never kissed anyone before. Can we do it again?"

He smiled, took her in his arms, and kissed her gently. He was still holding her when they heard the distant boom of Isaac's fowling piece. "We'd better build that fire Isaac asked for," Dave said.

Joseph Brant was waiting impatiently for the two young men when they returned to the house. Ordinarily he would have been pleased to see them burdened under such an abundance of meat for winter storage, but now he dismissed the ducks and geese with scarcely a glance.

"Hang them in the barn," he said, "and be quick about it. We are late already. Both of you get blankets and gear for a trip."

Isaac obeyed his father without a word, but Dave hesitated. He didn't want to see so much meat spoil. The birds ought to be cleaned immediately.

"They won't last, sir," he said, pointing to the ducks and geese.

"Never mind," Brant said brusquely. "I'll send somebody from the fort to take care of them."

He didn't tell them what was on his mind until they came in sight of the fort, after they had followed him at a stiff pace down-river. Dave and Isaac were puffing for breath when Brant finally checked his stride. They could see a string of bateaux loading at the docks in the river, with two lines of red-coated soldiers passing between the bateaux and the warehouses of the post commissary. At that distance the soldiers looked like red ants hurrying between their hill and a newly found food supply.

Brant spoke evenly, without a catch in his voice, as if he were fully rested instead of having just trotted four miles without stopping. "A runner has come in from Major Ross," he said. "They ran into a fight at Johnstown. Do you know a Continental officer named Willett, David?"

Dave nodded. Marinus Willett was the man chiefly responsible for the defense measures that had lately succeeded in limiting raiders to hit-and-run attacks.

"I know Colonel Willett of old," Brant said. "He jumped Ross and Butler at Johnstown. He's a sly fox, but he's a fighter too. The runner says it's likely they had to pull out and run for it. They were outnumbered and their supplies were gone. There was a storm brewing when Ross sent the runner. It hit us three days ago, so they must have caught it when they were in the deep woods north of the valley."

Isaac ventured a question in Mohawk. "North? Why would they not return the way they went in, by way of the lake of the Oneidas?"

"The runner says Willett has cut them off. When he came through, he saw militia in the valley beyond the German Flats. He brought Ross's word that they would swing north and head for Oswego. It's rough country up there. The woods are thick, and they may have to go through the foothills of the mountains. They'll be starving when they get to Oswego." He paused and added, "If they get there. In any case, we're going to Oswego with food and clothing for them."

"What about the Indians?" Isaac said. "Surely there are plenty of deer in that country, and lots of other game too. They can bring in some food for the army."

Brant's lip curled in scorn. Abruptly he said in Mohawk, "All the brave warriors that Guy Johnson sent with them scattered when the fighting started. They're spread out all over the country. Ross has no Indians to hunt game for him, and maybe none to guide him out of the woods. We may have to go find him, wherever he is. No more talk. Let's go."

The bateaux were fully loaded when they reached the docks. Grim-faced Rangers manned the oars. Joseph Brant climbed into the first bateau, motioning David and Isaac to follow him. Colonel Butler was already in the boat. His stern features were drawn with concern, and he shouted sharp orders to the Rangers who were preparing to embark. Colonel Guy Johnson and Brigadier Powell were standing on the dock, superintending the final stowing of the supplies.

A minute or so after Brant joined him, Colonel Butler looked at the other bateaux, twelve in all, and lifted his arm as a signal to cast off.

"Good luck to you!" General Powell called. Guy Johnson waved his arm. Butler and Brant nodded in reply. The first bateaux swung out into the current.

Dave Harper was pleased to find Sam Hawkins in the first bateau with Mr. Goring. They had time for only a few whispered words of greeting, because Goring, with his usual nervous excitement, was vainly trying to find some order in the long list of supplies that had been tumbled into the dozen bateaux.

"Did you hear that Ross and Walter Butler got

whipped?" Sam whispered excitedly. "Willett done it at Johnstown! I heard they lost most of their men running through the woods."

Dave nodded. "Brant told Isaac and me about it."

"Last the runner seen of them," Sam continued, "they was leggin' it into the woods with five hundred of our boys after 'em."

"Hawkins!" Goring exclaimed. "What's this you've written here? Four hundred k-m. What does that mean?"

"Four hundred pounds of corn meal, sir," Sam answered hastily.

"How many times, Hawkins, do I have to tell you that 'corn' is spelled with a *c*? Where is it? Which boat?"

"You're sittin' on it, sir," Sam answered, hiding a grin.

Goring lifted his coattails hastily. "So I am," he said. "Indeed I am."

They left Niagara far behind as the afternoon wore along. Watching the shore line glide past in the gray distance, Dave thought that this at last might be the chance to escape. Sam was with him, and they were going eastward to Oswego. He seethed with inner excitement as he pictured a dozen possibilities that might arise in the next few days. He would have to stay alert every minute or the opportunity might come suddenly and be gone before he and Sam could seize it. He wished that he could talk to Sam about it, but Goring's presence prevented that.

It was heavy work for the Rangers to pull the bateaux into the sweep of a northeast wind that was bitterly cold. Spray and occasional showers of rain coated the boats with a film of ice. The men's hands were raw and numb, and they kept the collars of their heavy coats pulled high to protect their necks and faces. Dave and Sam took their

turns at the oars. There was little conversation and no
laughter as the afternoon grew darker and colder. Rolling
waves thumped an endless rhythm against the bows of the
clumsy bateaux, and they tossed and pitched whenever
the wind shifted a few degrees. Water sloshed about the
men's feet. Long before Colonel Butler signaled the flotilla
to shore in the gathering darkness, every man was soaked
and shivering.

CHAPTER FIFTEEN

The two days following were bright and sunny, but there was little warmth in the wind that blew down out of Canada. The lake was choppy and the men were never dry because every wave that broke against the line of bateaux drenched the rowers with chilling spray.

It was midmorning of their fourth day out from Niagara, with no opportunity for David to talk to Sam about his hopes for escape, when the abandoned fort at Oswego came into sight. The Rangers lifted a ragged cheer of relief when Butler pointed to it, waving the bateaux to shore.

There was no sign of life other than a flight of canvasbacks and pintails feeding near the mouth of the Oswego River. The ducks took to the air at the approach of the flotilla. They swept out to the lake in a long line, their wings whistling softly as they flew overhead.

The party camped on the shore near the fort. The old works were overgrown with brush and high grass. British garrisons had been stationed there only briefly during the war. The Rangers set to work with their usual efficiency, building lean-to shelters and pitching the officers' tents. Brant and Colonel Butler stood on one of the bastions of the old fort, holding a council of war with the several

Ranger officers. When it was finished, Brant called to him the five Mohawks who were with the party and indicated with a wave of his hand that Isaac and Dave were to join him.

"We will go north and east to look for them," he said grimly. "They should have been waiting here for us. They are probably carrying their wounded and sick through the woods."

All afternoon the scouting party followed the game trails through the wilderness, making an elliptical swing eastward, then north, and finally westward again without finding a sign other than the ashes of campfires left by Oneida hunters in months gone by. Dave was amazed at the skill of the Mohawks in reading signs as they trotted through the trees. They seldom stopped or even slowed down, yet nothing passed their notice. They pointed to signs of deer that Dave, good hunter that he was, would probably have missed. Turned leaves in the underbrush, shale disturbed by sharp hoofs, a few hairs clinging to the bark of a fallen tree, a sapling twenty yards off the trail where a buck had rubbed his horns—all these and many more signs were pointed out by the warriors. One of them, trotting at Dave's side on a wide deer run, suddenly looked to his right at the summit of a ridge that ran beside the trail. Dave followed his gaze just in time to see the white flag of a deer bobbing out of sight in the brush on the ridge. Had the Mohawk been hunting, Dave thought, he would have stalked the deer and killed him, and I didn't even know he was there.

The Mohawks insisted that there were no men nearby. The game had been undisturbed for a long time, they told Brant. A party the size of Major Ross's force would have scattered the forest creatures many miles around them. Under Brant's questioning they kept pointing north, telling him that Ross must be many miles away in that direction. When the sun started to go down, the scouting party returned to the camp by the river, trotting the last few miles in darkness. Dave and Isaac were exhausted and footsore from the effects of the grueling pace that Joseph Brant had maintained all afternoon, but the Mohawk chief himself seemed scarcely tired. He reported his failure calmly to Colonel Butler.

"Not a sign of them, John," he said. "The Mohawks would have seen something if it had been there. They say Ross must be north, somewhere along the lake shore."

Colonel Butler showed his concern. "They have maps and compasses. Rangers shouldn't get lost."

"Willett may have chased them farther than we figured," Brant answered. "They might have gone as far north as the Black River."

Butler shook his head grimly. "Walter knows this country. So do Dan Millard and Dochstadter. They wouldn't get lost, even without Indians to bring them in."

"I'll make another try in the morning," Brant said. "This time we'll go farther north along the lake shore and then head east. The Mohawks say that if they were guiding the party they'd head straight across country to the lake from West Canada Creek and then come down here."

"They should know, Joseph," John Butler said. "I hope they're not in worse shape than we imagined. I'll send out some Rangers tomorrow besides your party."

That night Sam Hawkins was directed to sleep in the tent that held most of the food supplies, to protect them from woods marauders—raccoons, skunks, and bears.

These forest thieves would surely be drawn to the camp by the smell of food.

Dave asked Brant's permission to stay with his friend, which was granted without comment. He hoped he would have a chance to tell Sam what he'd been thinking all through the journey about striking through the woods for Stanwix. This might be the opportunity to escape they'd been waiting for.

On his way through the camp Dave noticed that Rangers were posted on sentry duty every forty yards around the perimeter of the campsite. It would be difficult, maybe impossible, to get past them. They would have to think of some way to get out of camp without causing suspicion.

Mr. Goring was also spending the night in the food tent. He was exhausted by the trip and fretful because he was far from the order and discipline of Niagara. He was also worried about the possibility of damage to his precious stores. He wasn't a woodsman, but he knew the damage that one bear could do in an hour. He tried to stay awake to help protect the food, but fatigue was stronger than worry, and he was soon snoring under blankets spread across the sacks of corn meal.

After he had fallen asleep, Dave and Sam started a whispered conversation.

"You think Willett wiped 'em out or captured the whole kit and caboodle of 'em?" Sam asked.

"No," Dave said. "He might have caught the Britishers, but not the Rangers. Once they're in the woods, they can take care of themselves."

"How come you didn't find 'em, then? They had plenty of time to get here from Johnstown."

"Maybe they've got a lot of wounded and sick," Dave

said. "They're out there somewhere. Daniel Morgan himself couldn't catch 'em in the woods, let alone Willett."

"Just the same," Sam said, "he must have give them an awful trimmin' if that runner that come to Niagara was tellin' the truth."

"Colonel Butler is worried," Dave agreed.

"Time was," Sam said thoughtfully, "that we sat in the forts and let 'em go where they pleased in the valley. It's been different lately. Our boys can whip 'em if they can catch 'em. You think that means we're winnin' the war, Dave?"

"We're winning it out here," Dave said. "No telling what's happening with Washington and the army." He listened carefully to Goring's snores, making sure that they were the long measured breathing of a sleeping man. "Sam, you know where this place is?"

"Sure," Sam answered. "Oswego, on the Oswego River. Where else?"

"That's not what I mean. You know how many miles it is from here to Stanwix?"

"No," Sam said, puzzlement in his voice. "Why you ask that? How far is it?"

"It's only seventy miles, Sam. Seventy miles—less than two days away."

"Might as well be a thousand," Sam answered, losing interest. "Don't do us any good for it to be so close."

"Maybe it will," Dave said quietly. "I've been picturing what's going to happen when Ross and his army get here. The place will be in an uproar, Sam. They'll have so many things on their minds, they'll never give us a thought. There'll be wounded and sick men to look after, and conferences among the officers, and plans to make for the trip back to Niagara or over to Buck's Island. They'll be busier than fleas in a militia barracks, Sam."

Sam lifted himself from his couch of bundled uniforms, resting on both elbows. He stared at Dave, seeing his friend's face dimly in the reflected glow of the campfires. He could make out the determined set of Dave's features, softened somewhat by the smile that touched his mouth.

"I know what you mean," he said. "You figger we should run while all the hooraw is going on." He paused. "You figger Hannah'll be waitin' for you at Stanwix, Dave?"

"I know she is," Dave said excitedly. "Just seventy-odd miles, Sam, and I'll see her again! This is the best chance we'll ever have. With four hours' start we can beat them to Stanwix. I know we can!"

"Maybe you can, Dave. You know the woods and all. Besides," Sam added unhappily, "I ain't much of a runner."

"You don't know what you can do until you have to do it," Dave said. "You want to stay at Niagara until the end of the war?"

"I dunno," Sam said. "I sure was anxious back at Niagara to get away, wasn't I? But now I'm faced with it, I'm scared. Maybe we'd be better off to wait."

"No man is ever better off as a prisoner than he would be free. What do you say, Sam? Will you try it with me? I don't want to go without you."

"They'll be watchin' us," Sam said. "They won't give us a chance to get off."

"When that army comes in, nobody is going to have any time to pay attention to us."

"I ain't sayin' you wouldn't make it alone, Dave. Maybe you better go by yourself. I'd only hold you back."

"Seventy miles, Sam! A four-hour running start and they'd never catch us."

"Let's sleep on it, Dave. We'll see how it looks tomorrow. We got to wait until the army gets here, anyways."

The scouting parties were delayed in their departure the next morning by the arrival of a bateau from Buck's Island at the foot of the lake. The bateau had been sent out to look for Ross and his men. It had been scouting the bays and inlets of the lake shore for the returning raiders. The men in the bateau, members of Sir John Johnson's Royal Regiment of New York, reported that Buck's Island had had no word from Major Ross since his departure. Using the same projected timetable as the force from Niagara, the Buck's Island people had decided that Ross should have brought his men to the lake by this time. They knew nothing of the battle at Johnstown and had been expecting Ross to return by way of Oneida Lake and the Oswego River.

Under questioning by Colonel Butler, the sergeant in charge of the bateau admitted they'd made only cursory inspection of the shore line on their way down from Buck's Island, since they expected Ross to be camped at Oswego.

"You'd better go north just as you planned, Joseph," John Butler said. "I'll send Rangers east and northeast. They're out there somewhere. They've got to be!"

Brant gave orders to his Mohawks to prepare themselves for at least three days in the woods. Dave was disturbed by these orders, because Ross might come into camp while the scouting party was out, and then the expected excitement would be gone by the time Brant came back.

While the scouts were packing supplies furnished by

Mr. Goring, there was a shout from a group of Rangers at the river's edge. They were pointing excitedly to the brushy perimeter of the forest in the northeast beyond the fort. Three men came out of the trees, limping and stumbling. The three figures halted when they saw the camp, shading their eyes to study it. Then they started a staggering run toward the river.

"They are here," Joseph Brant said simply, watching impassively as almost every man in camp ran out to meet the three newcomers.

As soon as he could, Dave edged away from Isaac Brant and stepped close to Sam. "Stay with me as much as you can," he whispered. "We'll get a chance to run before the day is gone."

The three men, all Rangers, were led into camp by the crowd. They were in sorry shape. Their uniforms were in shreds, two of them were unarmed, and they were all gaunt and bearded. Men crowded around them, offering them bits of food. They wolfed whatever was handed them, shaking their heads at the flood of questions.

Their flesh was ripped and scratched by brush, and their boots were held together by strips of cloth tied around them. When they'd eaten everything in sight, a Ranger officer interfered, ordering that they be given no more food lest they get sick. At the order, one of them began to cry. The other two, under questioning by the officer, said they were the scouts for the main force, a half mile or so behind them. Colonel Butler, ordering the mob to stand back, put an end to the hundreds of questions being fired at the men from all sides.

One of Dr. Guthrie's assistants took the three men in

charge, promising them more food and something hot to drink.

"Leave them alone now," Colonel Butler shouted. "No more questions."

A dozen Rangers left the camp at a dead run, to guide the rest of the raiders to the river.

"If they're the scouts," Dave heard Colonel Butler say to Brant, "then the good Lord only knows what condition the rest of them are in."

Brant nodded. "My Mohawks were right," he said. "They're coming in from the north along the lake shore. That's why we missed them yesterday."

Colonel Butler didn't answer. He was staring at the wilderness from which Ross's small army would soon emerge. His face was strained by worry, and his lips were a thin colorless line.

Fifteen minutes later a column of scarecrows came stumbling out of the woods. Leading them was a tall officer in a red coat, accompanied by another in the green and buckskin of the Rangers. Dave imagined that the British officer was Major Ross, while he easily recognized Captain Millard's limping stride. Behind them straggled Rangers and redcoats, marching without any attempt at keeping a column file. Some were leaning on staffs as they lurched along. Others were being helped by their companions. All of them were bearded, dirty, and tattered. Their faces, even at a distance, were seen to be drawn by hunger and exhaustion. Almost every man in the camp ran forward to help them. Colonel Butler and Joseph Brant stood alone, watching the scene. Dave, Isaac, and Sam stood nearby.

Colonel Butler put his hand above his eyes. He peered

at the column, which was now almost entirely clear of the forest. His voice, usually so quick and decisive, was halting when he spoke to Brant. "I don't see Walter there, Joseph. Can you make him out?"

Brant hesitated a second or two. "No, sir, I don't."

Butler put his hand down, but he still stared rigidly at the ragged column. "He's bringing up the rear, I expect," he said in controlled tones.

Another ten seconds passed, and suddenly the last of the raiders was out of the trees, lurching across the open ground. Ross and Millard were now only fifty yards away.

Colonel Butler continued to stare at the men. Dave watched the stiff features and tight lips. For only an instant—so quickly that it almost passed unnoticed—a shudder shook Butler's body, and his face relaxed in an instant of acute pain. Then he turned his head and looked into Brant's eyes. "He's not there, Joseph."

"No, John, he's not."

"He didn't come back. My boy didn't come back."

Butler passed his hands swiftly across his face. The young men, a few feet away, heard a low cry escape his lips. Then in a sudden transformation he became the commander of the Rangers once more. "Let us go to hear what the major has to say, Joseph."

Before they reached Ross, however, Captain Millard stepped swiftly forward. Sergeant Petry, stricken with sorrow, followed him, brushing tears from his eyes. Dan Millard limped to a halt before Colonel Butler. He spoke brokenly, anguished eyes looking into Butler's. "He's dead, sir. Walter is dead."

Colonel Butler nodded slowly several times. His voice was almost a whisper. "You were there, Daniel?"

"Yes, sir. At the ford on West Canada Creek, where they jumped us. We were holding them across the creek when it happened."

"Did you bring his——" Colonel Butler paused and then said, "Did you bring him with you?"

Millard broke down. His control left him and he put his hands across his eyes. He was crying in great racking sobs. He and Walter Butler had been friends since boyhood.

"Daniel! Daniel, take hold, now," Butler said softly. "Come now, my boy."

Millard managed to speak again. "We had to leave him, sir. They were crossing the creek."

"I know," Butler said. "You had enough to do to get here yourselves."

Sergeant Petry spoke up. "I had to pull Captain Millard away from the captain's body, sir. There was nothin' we could do. Their Injuns, Oneidas, was halfway across the creek when we left."

"Thank you, Petry," Butler said. "I know you did your best. Take care of Captain Millard." He turned to Brant, speaking wearily. "Bring Ross to see me later, Joseph. I want to be alone for a while. See that these poor fellows are taken care of."

The word of Walter Butler's death had spread immediately through the camp. The men who had come with Colonel Butler from Niagara stood silently as his straight figure passed among them. He walked to the bank of the river, where he stood for a long time at the edge of the water, staring into the distance where the blue waves of Lake Ontario merged with the cold gray sky of November.

The raiders had other news to tell. John Dochstadter

was dead. He had died of fever in the wilderness after the crossing of West Canada Creek.

When he heard that, Dave Harper thought of Catherine with deep pity, knowing that her mother would now return to the Indian way of life. Catherine would be drawn into her mother's family and would live according to Indian customs and traditions. Her white blood had died with her father in the dark northern forest. There was no one else to whom she could turn.

Joseph Brant brought the final important piece of news. He spent some time in serious conference with Ross, Millard, and several other officers of the expedition. Then he left them and returned to the evergreen lean-to that Isaac had built the day before. Dave, Sam, and Isaac were working over a fire before the lean-to, helping to cook the quantities of food that were needed for the starving raiders.

They saw Brant approaching, walking with a slow step that was foreign to his active nature. He seemed to be plodding along like an old man of seventy. His hands swung limply at his sides. His broad shoulders were slumped. When he was near enough, they could see that his eyes were dull and lifeless. Dave knew that it was not the deaths of Walter Butler, John Dochstadter, and the other men who had not returned that had so affected Brant. Rather, it must have been something that Ross and the others had told him. Isaac, too, knew that something was wrong. He stepped forward to meet his father, saying quietly in Mohawk, "What is it, Thayendanegea? Are you ill?"

Brant managed a grim smile. He rested his hand for a

few seconds on Isaac's shoulder. "Not ill, my son. I wish that were all."

Dave Harper, watching the chief, remembered how he had likened Brant to an eagle—powerful, fierce, indomitable. Now the power and the pride seemed to have been stripped away, and Brant was an ordinary man, suffering from some fearful blow.

"Can you tell me, my father?" Isaac said.

Brant nodded without answering. He slumped to a log that lay before the fire, sighing wearily. He held his hands to the blaze to warm them. He didn't speak for a while, but when he did his voice was quiet and steady. "You know well why we have fought in this war, Isaac. I have always known that the British Government is the only protector that the Long House has. Sir William used to warn me that powerful men in the colonies had their eyes on the rich lands of the Six Nations.

"When the war came, I believed that the future of the Long House, all its wealth and power, was at stake. We had to take the British side."

"I know all this, Father," Isaac said. "I think all our people know why we fight."

"We have won some battles and have harassed the rebels on their frontiers, destroying the food that their General Washington so badly needed. We forced him to send troops against us. When Sullivan and his army came into the lake country, we had a picture of what the future might be."

"This is not news, Father," Isaac said impatiently.

"Listen, my son. You have heard me say that if we lost, if the British lost, the Six Nations would soon be driven to Canada. I have predicted that all of the nations would lose their vast lands, as the Mohawks have already lost theirs in the valley. I have said many times that if we lose the war the Long House will be destroyed."

The three young men listened in silence, their eyes fixed on Brant's sad face. He paused, and finally Isaac spoke again. "Tell us what it is. What news did you hear?"

"Cornwallis has surrendered."

The words meant nothing to his listeners. Isaac looked puzzled. Sam turned wonderingly to Dave, who shrugged his shoulders to show that he knew no more than Sam did. Dave remembered that Cornwallis was a British general with a high reputation who had been campaigning in the south. It had been so long since the prisoners had thought of the progress of the war in other parts of the country that the news that Cornwallis had surrendered had no significance. The last time Dave had heard the name was just before his capture, when report had come that Daniel Morgan had whipped the redcoats at a place called The Cowpens, wherever that might be.

"Who is Cornwallis?" Isaac asked.

"The last British hope of crushing the rebellion," Joseph Brant replied. "He has surrendered his entire army to Washington and the French somewhere in Virginia. Major Ross has the details. You will hear them soon enough."

Dave ventured a question. "You mean, sir, that the war is over?"

Brant shook his head with a grim smile. "No, David. We will fight on. We can do nothing else. But we cannot win. The King's ministers will never send another army to America—not after five years of winning battles but somehow losing armies. First Burgoyne and now Cornwallis. They won't give another general the chance to sur-render."

Dave and Sam looked at each other briefly, exchanging quick flashes of relief and triumph. After so many years of fighting and running away, now Washington had the British on the run!

"What will we do now, Father?" Isaac asked soberly.

"Some of our Mohawks are already settled in Canada. The rest must follow them. We will be the first of the nations to go, but I can see the time when all the Indians of the Long House will live on the other side of the St. Lawrence, and our lands will be taken by the white men. They have been looking westward for many years. They covet these lands, and they mean to have them. When they've finished the war, they'll come. We can't stand alone against them. When they come, the Indian must go. It is the end of the Long House."

"Can't we fight for what is ours?" Isaac asked fiercely.

Brant shook his head sadly. "We can talk as loudly and as often as we may, Isaac. We may drive a better bargain for the land." He looked at Dave. "Remember that young Seneca you saw at Buffalo Creek, David?"

"The one with the red coat?"

"Yes, Red Jacket. We have need of his kind now. Talk-ers, not fighters. The days of Hiokatoo and Little Beard and Tall Chief and Hot Bread and the days of Joseph Brant are done."

Isaac clenched his fists. "You are the war chief, Father. You are the leader. Won't you fight as you always have?"

Brant stood up, lifting a quieting hand to Isaac. "Fight, my son? Yes, we'll fight as long as the British fight with us. Think for a minute. Two years ago Sullivan came with five thousand men. When the British leave us, Washington could send him back with ten thousand. Twenty thousand! What could our fifteen hundred or two thousand warriors do against so many? No, my son. As soon as the war is over—and that will be soon now—we will start talking." Brant smiled bitterly. "Red Jacket and his silver tongue talked a great many warriors away from battle with Sullivan two years ago. But now we have a use for him and his oratory. My day is over, Isaac. Look to Red Jacket. Look to the talkers. They will be the leaders."

CHAPTER SIXTEEN

Dave and Sam, by talking to some of the Rangers who had returned with Ross, pieced together the story of the raid and its aftermath. After Ross and his force had reached the valley by way of Oneida Lake, they had taken a southerly route, keeping to the big woods, until they were far into the ring of settlements. Then they struck the village of Warrensbush and the farms around it. The village was close to Schenectady and heretofore had been untouched by war parties. Leaving Warrensbush in flames, they had crossed the river to Johnstown. They intended to burn barns, granaries, and storehouses all along the northern bank of the Mohawk in a swift, fiery retreat back to Oneida Lake and the bateaux they had hidden on its shores.

Willett, however, had learned the ways of war parties in his years of chasing raiders in the Mohawk Valley. He struck swiftly with Continentals and militia that had seemed to pour in from every part of the valley. He crossed to Johnstown with a force that was the equal of Ross's little army. Reinforcements joined him every hour. After the engagement in Johnstown, where the raiders had suffered severely and where the Indians had deserted the field, Ross had been obliged to head into the wilderness on a path that would take him far north of Oneida Lake. If he tried to head for the lake, Willett could intercept him at any point.

For three days, during which the few Indians left with the army deserted, Ross and Walter Butler had pushed their men toward West Canada Creek. Willett, they were sure, would not follow them beyond the creek. He couldn't carry enough supplies and still keep the speed necessary for successful pursuit.

The weather was bitterly cold and blustery, promising a storm. The storm came, and upon its heels, like the timber wolves that gathered on the snow-covered hills, came Willett's hardened veterans. They were led by Oneida Indian scouts, who had hunted the Canada Creek country all their lives and knew every foot of its pine-covered slopes and rocky ravines.

It was a running battle in the storm, with Willett's men harrying the fleeing Rangers and redcoats. Ross and Butler kept the men moving for the creek and the safety it promised.

Walter Butler had seen the regulars and Rangers safely across the ford, and he and Daniel Millard, with a few Rangers, were holding the ford in a final rear-guard action. The last shot of the engagement had tumbled Butler from his horse, and he died in Daniel Millard's arms.

What was left of Ross's force made its weary journey to Lake Ontario. Horse meat and a few sacks of corn had kept them from starving.

The rescue party from Niagara had performed its mission well by having food, clothing, and medical aid ready for Ross's men when they came out of the wilderness, but the camp on the shore of the Oswego River was a grim scene for the rest of that day. There were a dozen wounded men for Dr. Guthrie, the Rangers' medical officer, to care for, and twice that many were seriously ill. The doctor did his best, but one man died before noon, and there wasn't much hope for some of the others. Dave and Sam were put to work with a squad of Rangers to prepare four of the bateaux for an immediate return to Niagara, carrying the wounded and the sick.

The meaning of Cornwallis' surrender at Yorktown had spread quickly among the troops, and as Dave and Sam worked with the Rangers, they heard man after man agree that the war was over for them. There was a quiet bitterness in the words of these men who had fought a lonely war, neglected and sometimes forgotten by the King's ministers in London. They knew the meaning of defeat. They faced exile in a foreign country for the rest of their lives. Most of them were from the Mohawk Valley and the Susquehanna settlements in Pennsylvania. Time and again, as they discussed the pattern of the future, they compared the land they were going to live in with the country from which they had been driven.

It was difficult for Dave and Sam, listening to the conversations around them, to conceal their elation as they began to realize that the long years of raiding were finished, that the days when frontier settlements lived in constant fear of firebrand, tomahawk, and scalping knife were gone and would never return.

To Dave Harper, even though his mind was full of his immediate plan to escape to the country that most of these men would never see again, there was real tragedy in their quiet sorrow. He listened with warm compassion when

Jacob Bowman began to tell the others about his boys in Pennsylvania. He asked if any of them thought it possible that his wife might leave her rebel family and come to Canada when the fighting was done. None of them answered Bowman.

He persisted. "Don't you think she'd come on up here if she knew I had a couple hundred acres and a house?"

"Don't you take on, Jake," said another Ranger, a former neighbor of Bowman, whose name was Shingorlan. "You and me will go down there and get those young'uns of yours and bring 'em back to Canada."

"They hate me now, I s'pose," Bowman said listlessly. "They been taught to hate me. Two sons I got, only little fellers, and they'll grow up hatin' their own father."

"Maybe you're wrong, Jake," said Shingorlan awkwardly. "You get you a nice big farm in Canada and fix you up a good house and all, and then you send for her and the boys. Blood is thicker'n water, Jake."

"No, it ain't," harshly interrupted a gaunt Ranger from Ross's raiders, who was nursing a shattered arm from a musket wound at West Canada Creek. He was waiting to take his place in one of the bateaux. "I can tell you it ain't. Down to Johnstown, when we was shootin' at the rebels, I seen my father's brothers, my own two blood uncles, pointin' to me and aimin' square at me. It was just like Oriskany, four years ago, when we was all shootin' at relatives and neighbors."

"Well, it's all over now," Shingorlan said. "We lost it, and now we got to pay for losing. The losers always pay the reckoning."

The wounded man nodded and spit into the water. "Canada," he muttered disgustedly. "My wife is sure goin' to lift my hair when she hears we can't go back home to Schoharie. She'll blame me for losin' the hull durn war. She can't stand them cold winters."

"Two hundred acres, that's what I heard they'll give us," said another man dolefully. "I had five hundred in Northumberland. Good bottom land along the river."

Colonel Butler and Joseph Brant interrupted the men's talk of the future by arriving to supervise the embarkation of the sick and wounded. Dr. Guthrie, his round face marked with lines of worry, was arranging litters for the men no longer able to walk. The Rangers at the boats fell silent as Butler and Brant reached them. They watched Colonel Butler with open curiosity, wondering how their hard-bitten commander was taking the loss of his son.

Butler's face was as stern and his eyes were as keen as ever when they surveyed the details of the loading, but Dave Harper could see that the shock of his son's death had taken its due. John Butler looked old and weary. To see the two most resourceful and feared frontier leaders of the British forces bearing the burden of their knowledge that their power was broken was the surest gauge of the importance of the news from Yorktown. Dave Harper thrilled with pride and happiness as he imagined the wild celebrations that must have erupted all over the colonies when news of the victory had arrived.

Brant said a few words to Butler, and the colonel nodded. "All right, men. Into the boats and on your way. Make all the speed you can, but be easy with the sick men."

Joseph Brant called Dave and Sam to him. "You two will go with them. You can be more useful to Dr. Guthrie than you can be here."

The words were a shock to Dave. He had already decided to try to escape from the camp just after nightfall. He and Sam could have run all night long on the good trail toward Oneida Lake. With a few hours' start, he was sure they could outdistance any Rangers sent in pursuit, and there were no Indians in the camp who could be sent after them. He tried to hide his chagrin, but Brant saw that something was wrong. He looked speculatively at Dave. "You cannot stay with me," he said quietly. "Isaac and I will not be here more than another few hours. We are taking a journey. It's best that you go back to Niagara, David."

"It's not that, sir," Dave said quickly, hoping he'd covered his disappointment. "Sam and I should help Mr. Goring with the supplies."

"I have already told Mr. Goring that you are going with the wounded," Brant said. "They need you more than he does. Into the first boat, now. They are ready to go."

The two young men walked toward the leading bateau.

"It was a good idea while it lasted," Sam whispered. "I was already tastin' my mother's rhubarb pie."

"We're not licked yet," Dave said grimly. "It's a long way to Niagara, and there are only a few Rangers going with us. We're not going to give up now, Sam. We'll never be this far eastward again. We're going to try it!"

Captain Daniel Millard was in command of the four bateaux. His old Cherry Valley wound had acted up during the flight through the wilderness, and Colonel Butler had decided that Millard wasn't equal to the march across country to Niagara.

Dave and Sam entered the first bateau and helped with the stepping of the mast. The wind was out of the northeast again, and the bateaux could sail before it as long as it held steady.

The four craft moved out into the waters of the lake with furled sails, propelled by Rangers at the oars. When they were well into the open water, the sails were set and swiftly the mouth of the Oswego River began to fall behind in the distance. The men were all silent. Only an occasional groan or cry from the wounded lifted above the sound of the waves slapping against the boats.

Daniel Millard motioned Dave to come to his side. "Well, Dave, you heard the news back there at Oswego?"

"About Captain Butler? Yes, I'm sorry for Colonel Butler. He seemed to take it hard."

"Walter was a good man, David," Millard said softly. "No matter what your friends say about him, he was a good man. Remember that when you hear the stories they'll tell about him."

"I will, Captain."

Millard stared across the open water. "I wish I wasn't the one to bring the news to Niagara. His mother is there. I'll have to tell her."

Dave said nothing. While all the people on the frontier must be rejoicing at the word that Walter Butler was dead, Dave could understand Daniel Millard's grief at the loss of his lifelong friend.

"The war will soon be over, Dave," Millard said finally. "You'll be glad of that, I imagine?"

"I'll be happy to get home."

"We'll miss you, Dave. You can stay, you know. There's land in plenty up in Canada."

"No, Captain," Dave said firmly.

"I suppose you're right. A man belongs in his own coun-

try. Canada is our country now. You'll always be welcome
if you come back to visit us."

"Thank you. I've made many friends at Niagara."

"Don't tell your countrymen that," Millard answered.
"They won't believe you."

The four boats made good time in the steady breeze,
in spite of their awkwardness under sail. By the time the
bleak November day was turning to dusk, they were well
along the lake shore from the mouth of the Oswego. Millard watched the shore line carefully until he directed the
steersmen to pull into a bay with a sandy beach. The bay
was protected on three sides by high wooded bluffs. After
the wounded and sick were fed and attended by Dr.
Guthrie, with Dave and Sam helping him, the rest of the
party made their meal. The Rangers gathered all the drift-
wood in sight, because it promised to be a cold night.
Once the wounded men were made comfortable by the
fires, the others rolled themselves in their blankets for the
night.

There were no sentries posted. None of the Rangers gave
any attention to the two prisoners. Sam was prepared to
make his bed as close to the heat of a campfire as he could
get, but Dave led him out of the firelight toward the base
of the bluffs. They spread their blankets in the sand and
pretended to go to sleep immediately. Most of the men
were already snoring. Only Captain Millard and Dr.
Guthrie were still active. They sat beside one of the drift-
wood fires that was built to burn slowly all night and re-
flect heat upon the sick and wounded who lay under the
upturned bateaux. Millard and Guthrie were smoking
pipes and conversing idly. Perhaps half an hour after

everyone else had turned in, they too rolled their blankets about them.

Dave lay on his side for a long time, anxiously watching the blanketed figures. There was no sign that any of them were awake. He could hear Sam's steady breathing.

"Shall we try it now, Dave?"

"Wait until we're sure they're all asleep," Dave answered. "They'd hear us climbing the cliff."

Dave's caution proved wise. A few minutes later Dr. Guthrie got to his feet and made a round of the wounded men. Another half hour went by before Dave put out his hand and touched Sam's shoulder. "Roll your blankets," he said softly. "We'll need 'em."

In a minute or so, working in the darkness, they both had their blankets rolled and slung from their shoulders on buckskin thongs cut from the thrums of Dave's hunting shirt. Stealthily they crawled toward the base of the bluff that bulked black against the sky. Hand over hand they went up the bluff, using rock projections and stunted shrubs for hand- and footholds. Each time either of them dislodged gravel or a chunk of rock, they froze against the bluff with eyes fixed on the camp below. There was no alarm, however, and not one of the sleeping figures moved. Even the wounded, some of whom had been moaning and crying all day, were silent.

In ten minutes' climbing they gained the lip of the bluff. Eastward the wilderness stretched in the darkness. Dave was glad to see that they had timed their climb perfectly, because the tip of the full moon was just edging above the treetops. In a few minutes the moonlight would be streaking among the bare trees to light the way.

They moved a few feet from the bluff and were on a

wide trail. It skirted the top of the bluff and followed the lake shore toward the Oswego River. During his months at Niagara, Dave had managed to imprint on his mind the details of the maps that were tacked to the wall in Joseph Brant's house. He remembered that this trail forked a few miles this side of Oswego. The left branch would take them right back to Colonel Butler's camp, but the right branch, whenever they found it, would lead them to Three Rivers and then to Oneida Lake. Once they reached the lake, he figured that they would be safe. They'd be only a few miles from Fort Stanwix.

They edged back to the bluff and looked down once more on the sleeping camp. None of the blanketed figures stirred.

"Let's go," Dave said.

They began to run eastward.

CHAPTER SEVENTEEN

Once clear of the bluff, Dave and Sam ran for fifteen minutes at a wild pace through the dark forest until they were so winded they had to stop for breath. The moonlight was just beginning to come through the trees, but there wasn't yet enough light to see the ground clearly. They were fortunate that the trail was wide and had been beaten smooth over many years by the feet of countless Indians. As it was, they tripped and stumbled many times during that first headlong run. Once Sam hit an ice-filled depression in the path and went flying on his face. Dave came back to help him, but Sam shook him off and stood for a few seconds, panting to catch his breath. Then they started to run again.

They finally stopped when they came to a brook that tumbled down the slope over ice-coated stones to the lake. They drank a few mouthfuls of the cold water, then lay on the bank for a few minutes until their gasping breath had returned to normal.

"We can't keep this up," Dave panted. "We'd better slow down to a steady trot. A fall could mean a broken arm or leg. You ever do much deer hunting, Sam?"

"Sure," Sam said. "The Catskills down by Kingston are

full of deer. I'll bet my brothers have been out near every day this fall."

"You know how fast you run when you're after a wounded deer in country that's fairly open? Sometimes you can see him ahead of you, and sometimes you're following the blood marks. You just keep going until you run him down. Well, that's the pace we ought to set for ourselves. A man, can go on for twelve hours that way if he has to."

"You start out ahead," Sam said. "I'll try to follow you. I ain't sayin' I can do it, though."

"If you can't make it, just holler and I'll stop."

"Nothin' doin', Dave," Sam said quickly. "If I have to call it quits, you go on. No reason why you should get caught again just because I can't keep up with you."

"You'll be all right," Dave said. "The first few miles are always the hardest. After that you get your breathing right and you just keep moving along."

They crossed the roaring brook on one of several great trees that Indians had felled to serve as bridges. On the other side Dave stretched his long legs into a steady, mile-consuming jog. The moon was climbing into the sky and a pale light filtered to the path.

Dave looked over his shoulder every hundred yards or so to see how Sam was faring. Evidently Sam had gained his second wind, because he was matching Dave stride for stride.

In some places where the undergrowth was thick or where tall evergreens blacked out the sky, Dave had to strain his eyes to follow the turns and twists of the trail. Luckily it was bordered by waist-high brush, and whenever he felt twigs and branches snapping against his body, he veered in the other direction. Roots, stones, and ice-filled holes were the worst problems. Time and again both he and Sam stumbled. A twisted ankle would end their hope of outdistancing pursuit. Dave concentrated on the trail at his feet to such an extent that he missed the fork in the path. He was halted a few yards beyond it by Sam's hail.

"Here's another path, Dave," Sam called, struggling for breath. "Goes to the right."

Dave came back to study as well as he could in the darkness the broad, hard-packed path that branched eastward. "This is it," he said. "Come on."

"Good thing I blundered into it," Sam said. "If we kept left, we'd of wound up in a campful of Butler's Rangers again."

"I think we'll be all right now," Dave said. "Some streams to cross, but I'm sure this trail goes straight ahead to Oneida Lake. We can follow the lake, go up Wood Creek, and then we're at Stanwix."

"You make it sound easy," Sam groaned. "I ain't goin' to live through the night."

They rested for two hours toward dawn, and then began to run again. The going was much easier now that they could see, and they made good time in spite of fatigue and stiff muscles. The next time they stopped for an hour's rest, when the sun was entering its high arc in the sky, Dave scouted the woods until he found a hickory sapling. He cut it with his hunting knife, the only weapon either of them had, and dragged it back to where Sam was lying on the ground.

"What's that for?" Sam asked puzzledly. "You think I'll be needing a cane before the day is out?"

"You'll see," Dave told him, grinning. "I won't tell you until I see if it will work."

He cut a length of the sapling about three feet long, trimmed it, and then split one end carefully with his knife blade. He worked the split back about six inches, and into it he pushed an oblong rock, binding it there with strips of buckskin from his hunting shirt. He also bound the split so it wouldn't move up the staff. The result was a rough facsimile of an Indian war club. He twirled it several times around his head, testing its balance. Then he let it fly through the air toward a nearby log. It sailed clumsily, end over end. He wasn't satisfied with its performance. He retrieved it, removed the rock, shortened the handle, and selected another rock for the head.

"You mind telling me what you're doing?" Sam demanded. "What's that thing for?"

"When did you get your first musket?" Dave asked, smiling.

"When I was thirteen," Sam said. "Why?"

"That was for deer and bear and such. How'd you hunt before that? Rabbits, squirrels, woodchucks?"

"With a sling," Sam answered. "All the boys had 'em. Weren't much good, though. You had to hit a rabbit square in the head to kill him."

"We didn't use slings back home in Cherry Valley," Dave said. He tested the balance of his new weapon. "We used these things. Called them hunting sticks. Watch, now."

Again he twirled the club above his head and let it fly at the stump. This time it was carried straight to its mark by the forward weight of the heavier rock. It struck the log with a thump, only a few inches from the spot where Dave had aimed it.

"Good enough," he said. "A piece of iron on the end is better, but this rock will do. Maybe we'll eat before we get to Stanwix."

They resumed the journey. Their bodies protested against the strain, and they had to make more frequent stops. Sam was obviously reaching the limit of his endurance, but he kept doggedly throwing one foot after the other. Dave watched his friend closely, calling a halt whenever Sam began to weave from one side of the path to the other.

He was anxious to get as far as possible from the camp on the lake shore before they stopped for a long rest but he restrained his impatience, remembering that Sam had not had the benefit of a summer's farming to toughen his muscles.

The hunting stick didn't fell any rabbits the first few times Dave tried it. Whenever the trail crossed a treeless natural clearing or a rocky ridge where vegetation had a chance to grow in the sunlight, he kept watch for the sudden startling rush of a frightened rabbit. Whenever he saw a white tail flashing through the brown cover, he twirled the stick and let it fly. This was a different kind of hunting, however, from that of his boyhood days. Then he had still-hunted, taking care to move slowly and carefully, with the result that the rabbits were apt to bound a few feet through the grass and then look foolishly to see what had startled them. Now, when his pounding feet put them out of cover, they ran for their lives as if a fox were after them, and so were out of range of the stick sometimes before he even saw them.

Shortly after noon Dave held up his hand as they entered a great expanse of maple forest, studded here and there with stands of black walnut trees. "Come on," he said to Sam. "There are squirrels in those walnuts. Let's see if we can get a meal."

They moved into a grove of walnuts, walking slowly and cautiously to avoid snapping the dry twigs that littered the ground. Suddenly a squirrel scampered across the ground and flitted out of sight, climbing the trunk of a tall tree. Dave saw his tail flick behind the first branch, about twenty feet off the ground.

Sam grinned and pointed to the other side of the tree. Circling carefully, he showed that he had done plenty of squirrel hunting. The squirrel was clinging to the far side of the tree and, as Sam came around, clawed his way around the trunk to stay out of sight of the moving figure.

Dave poised the hunting stick as Sam circled the tree. As Sam went one way, the squirrel went the other. In a few seconds it was right above Dave, its four feet spread and its body flattened against the trunk. The hunting stick whizzed through the air. It found its mark, and the squirrel fell with a thump among the leaves on the ground. They had food. One squirrel wasn't much, but it would keep them going. Maybe they'd get another.

Sam was all for skinning the squirrel right there and making a meal of it immediately, but Dave insisted they spare a few more minutes for hunting.

They walked through the grove, watching the ground and lower branches carefully. Almost immediately they saw a gray flash along the ground. A minute later they had another squirrel, knocked from a big walnut tree.

Then Dave made a discovery that was almost as rewarding as the two squirrels. He saw a walnut tree that was clawed and scraped as high as his arms could reach. A few feet above the claw marks was a huge, bulging knot in the tree trunk with a hole about four inches in diameter in its center.

"A bee tree," Dave exclaimed. "Look here, Sam! A bear has been trying to get up to the honey. Come on! Stand on my shoulders."

"Not me," Sam said quickly. "I don't want to get stung to death."

"They won't sting you in this weather," Dave said. "They're asleep for the winter. Come on. Dip in and get a few combs."

Reluctantly Sam climbed to Dave's shoulders and gingerly put his hand into the hole. "I feel 'em!" he said fearfully. "There's millions of 'em in here."

"They're not stinging you, are they?"

Sam admitted that the bees weren't bothering him. He withdrew his hand, holding a dripping yellow piece of comb. He dropped it into the leaves and kept probing until there was a sizable pile of honeycomb on the ground.

"That's enough," Dave said. "We can't carry any more. Besides, we have to eat and get going."

Sam got down and licked his fingers. "Man, that tastes fine! I don't blame that bear for tryin' to get to it."

"Let's hurry," Dave said. "You start skinning the squirrels while I wrap up this honey."

Dave cut the cape from his hunting shirt to make a bag for the dripping honeycomb.

"Will we eat these squirrels raw?" Sam asked. "You think we ought to risk a fire?"

"If they're after us, a fire isn't going to make any difference. As for time, we had a long start on 'em, and they can't run any faster than we can. I think we ought to cook 'em. The wind is blowing pretty well. Nobody will see the smoke, but they might smell it a mile away."

"If anybody is as close as a mile, we'll get caught, no matter what. Let's cook 'em. Besides, raw meat might make us sick."

Sam finished skinning the squirrels while Dave made a fire, using the flint and steel that he carried in the hunting pouch at his belt. He soon had a small hardwood blaze that didn't throw much smoke. They spitted the squirrels and seared them for a few minutes. Sam insisted on dripping honey over the meat, and they sucked at bits of honeycomb while it was cooking. They were so hungry that long before the flesh was cooked through they were tearing at it ravenously. Two squirrels were better than no squirrels at all, but they were still hungry when the last bit of flesh was gnawed from the bones. They cracked the slender bones to get the marrow in them.

"I could eat a half dozen more," Sam said unhappily. "That wasn't more'n a bite or two."

"Take some honeycomb to suck on while we're traveling. There's nothing like sugar to give you strength. Anyway, Sam, you'll eat your fill when we get to Stanwix," Dave added. "Let's go. We've come about twenty miles. I want to make fifteen more today."

Sam groaned. "I'll drop in my tracks, Dave. I just can't do it."

Dave jumped to his feet, wincing as his muscles flexed painfully. "We've got to keep our start on 'em," he said. "If Captain Millard had any Indians to send after us, I wouldn't stop at all. But Rangers will stop to eat and rest the same as we just did. And they can't run any faster than we can, Sam. Come on, now."

"My poor feet!" Sam cried as he pushed himself up. "They're raw. I'll wear 'em off before we get to Stanwix."

"You'll wear 'em off marching back to Niagara if we don't get started and keep going for the rest of the day. You ready now?"

"I guess I am, if you say so," Sam replied mournfully. "Ready as I'll ever be."

He was better than his word, however, because he kept doggedly at Dave's heels all day long.

They traveled until dusk, camping for the night on a height of land on the north shore of Lake Oneida. They were cold, hungry and exhausted. They ate most of the honey that was left, saving a few pieces of comb for breakfast, and in spite of their discomforts they fell asleep almost as soon as they rolled into their blankets. There was a light fall of snow during the night, but its cold touch on their faces didn't awaken them. They slept until the glow of dawn fell on the waters of the lake.

CHAPTER EIGHTEEN

They didn't reach Fort Stanwix on the second day. They hadn't turned off their course, because Dave recognized many landmarks they had passed going westward on this trail after they'd been captured in the spring. But with the absence of any sign of pursuit, and Sam's obvious inability to keep the pace of the day before, Dave called more frequent halts for rest and whatever food they could find. After many vain attempts the hunting stick finally knocked over a sitting rabbit, and they had another meal. They also managed to find hickory and beechnuts, as well as black walnuts, buried among the fallen leaves around the trees. An hour's hunting, however, would produce only enough nutmeats to make a mouthful, so thorough had the squirrels been in the few weeks that the nuts had been on the ground.

They camped on the second night at a stream that Dave remembered was not more than ten miles from Stanwix. He had been with several hunting and scouting parties the year before that had come farther than this from the fort.

He would have tried to press on to Stanwix in the darkness of the second night if he had been alone, but Sam was worn out. He was reduced to stumbling along on legs that had lost all their strength, so that he would have fallen flat on his face if his forward momentum hadn't carried him along with each step for the instant necessary to bring his other foot forward.

They were so near the fort in the morning that Dave decided to hunt for a half hour before waking Sam. Ten miles was a long way to go without food.

He went far afield from their camp in an effort to find a suitable clearing where rabbits might be feeding. He found such a place down the trail toward Stanwix, but just as he was about to push his way through the brush that bordered it he smelled smoke. He looked upward. A thin gray column curled into the still air from the far side of the clearing. His heart leaped. Perhaps it was a hunting or scouting party from Stanwix.

He pushed the brush aside eagerly, and through the aperture looked across the clearing. There was a campfire there, but men from Stanwix hadn't built it. Six Indians were crouched around it, eating their morning meal, and Dave eased himself back into the brush, his throat tight and dry. To have come so far and then meet Indians! He thought of the escape he had tried to make on the journey westward to Niagara. The same thing had happened. He had come so far, only to be captured.

On second thought, perhaps they were Oneidas! In that event, he could walk out into the clearing and greet them. There'd be food for him and for Sam, and friends to accompany them to the fort. He grinned. They must be Oneidas. No other Indians would be so close to a well-garrisoned American fort.

He parted the bushes again and looked across the clearing. He was wrong! Fear gripped him, and for a moment he almost gave himself away. He wanted to jump up and run. Whatever they were, they weren't Oneidas—he'd seen scores of Oneidas during his service at Stanwix. He was afraid the strange Indians had seen him, and he began to crawl swiftly back through the brush, his heart pounding as he waited for a triumphant whoop.

When none came, he regained his control. He realized he'd have to take another look at them, more carefully this time, to find out who they were. He moved the bushes slowly, just enough to see the camp across the clearing.

Five of these Indians wore crude fur clothing and head coverings of raccoon or muskrat fur. The sixth man, however, was bundled in a British military jacket so stained and dirty that its brilliant red color was gone forever.

After a moment's reflection Dave decided that these six were Missisaugas. A good part of the motley crew of Indians that Guy Johnson had sent with Ross had been Missisaugas, and these six, he supposed, were making their leisurely way west after abandoning Ross in the wilderness.

Apparently none of them had noticed the brush moving with his passage. He slid himself backward on the ground for a few yards before getting to his feet. Then he ran the half mile or so to the place were Sam lay sleeping.

"Wake up!" he said urgently, shaking Sam. "Come on, Sam. Wake up!"

"Lemme be, Dave," Sam groaned, trying to settle himself again in his blankets. "Almost there. No need to hurry now. Ain't nobody after us."

"Indians, Sam! Get up, will you!"

Sam was on his feet instantly, staring around him in fright and ready to run if Dave would only tell him which way to go.

"Injuns! Where are they?"

"Back toward Stanwix. Camped alongside the trail. We'll have to go through the woods to get around 'em."

"How many of 'em?"

"Six. They look like those Canadian Indians we saw at Niagara."

Dave led the way into the thick forest, heading as accurately as he could toward the clearing where they had been captured last winter. He traveled at a dangerous pace through the tangle of logs and briers and storm-broken branches. He realized that a few minutes after the Indians resumed their journey they would find the place on the trail where he and Sam had camped, and would then find the traces of their flight into the forest. They were sure to investigate such a fresh trail. Dave knew that speed was the only thing that could keep him and Sam from being captured, perhaps killed. He knew little about the Missisaugas, but they looked fierce. He and Sam had to get within sight of Fort Stanwix before the Indians caught up with them.

Dave made no attempt to hide the traces of their rough passage. To do so would be to waste time they badly needed. His best attempt to hide the trail would scarcely slow a trained tracker to a walk. Sam was able to keep close behind Dave on this run because Dave had to pick their route through the tangle, and all Sam had to do was follow. By leaving a plain trail, Dave knew he was adding to the speed of the Indians when they started in pursuit, but he hoped they would linger over their fire.

Obviously they were in no hurry to get back to Niagara, where there would be neither presents nor praise for them, if they were, as he thought, deserters from Ross's army. But that was another reason that made him sure they would follow a fresh trail made by two white men. To return to Niagara with two scalps would be far better than to go back with no trophies at all.

Dave and Sam ran for almost an hour, heading east by southeast toward the clearing that Dave was sure he could find. Once they were there, they could take the wagon road that led directly to the fort, two miles away. After an hour went by, when they were both exhausted, bleeding from bramble scratches and bruised by many falls on the uneven ground, Dave began to wonder if they had passed the clearing. It would be easy enough to make such an error if they were even slightly off course. He was about to head north in a desperate effort to go straight to the fort when suddenly he burst through the brush into the clearing. His direction hadn't been wrong; either they had been farther from Stanwix than he had believed, or they had made less speed through the dense forest than he supposed.

There were no signs of recent woodcutting operations in the clearing, but there was no reason to regard that as unusual. He was disappointed. He had held the faint hope of running into a party of woodcutters. They must be cutting wood in another of the several places near the fort where storm-felled, seasoned wood lay in abundance.

Dave and Sam ran along the wagon road, calling on their final reserves of strength for added speed now that they were so close to the protection of the fort. As Dave remembered the road, it twisted through the woods for slightly more than two miles before it left the trees on the plain near the fort. They had run perhaps half of that distance when they heard the first faint yell of the Missisaugas on the back trail. The Indians must have reached the clearing.

"Can't go on!" Sam gasped. "You go, Dave."

Dave turned and took Sam's arm in a strong grip. "Only a mile," he cried. "They won't dare come too close. Hang onto me!"

They went on for ten minutes more, in a staggering run that seemed agonizingly slow to Dave. An occasional yell drifted to them through the still air, each one closer than the one before. Dave kept looking back, intending to put out a last desperate effort when it was needed. Just as the first Indian came into sight, so did the plain and the fort. With his free arm, Dave pointed wildly at the high palisade and the bastions of the sprawling fortress, yelling incoherently to Sam, who managed a feeble, twisted grin.

They dashed onto the open plain. Dave looked back, expecting to see the Indians stop and turn back. Instead, they were coming ahead as fast as ever. Dave then watched the great gates of Stanwix as he stumbled along, railing at the stupidity of the sentries who hadn't yet swung a sally port open. He wanted to see a flood of blue-clad Continentals pour out to take care of those Indians.

He yelled as loudly as his straining lungs permitted. There was not a sign of the garrison, nor any other living thing. There should have been smoke rising in the still air, but there was none. There should have been cannon poking their snouts through embrasures in the bastions, but he could see none. Dave threw another quick glance over his shoulder. He was amazed to see that the Missisaugas had not given up the chase. They were bunched about forty yards away, yelling in triumph.

Dave realized suddenly and with overwhelming despair that Fort Stanwix was deserted. There was no garrison to come out to rescue them. Sam had been desperately watching the fort too. He understood, a few seconds after Dave, that the fort was empty. He gave up. They were thirty yards from the gates when Sam groaned and stopped running, and fell heavily to the ground. Dave tried to haul him to his feet.

Suddenly the air was torn by the wild, fierce sound of a Mohawk war cry. The Missisaugas skidded to an abrupt stop, staring at the gate of the fort. Dave looked wonderingly at them and then turned to see what had halted them. He expected to see soldiers come through the gates.

Instead, Joseph Brant stood beside the open sally port, Isaac behind him, holding a leveled musket. Brant had a pistol in each hand, muzzles directed toward the Missisaugas.

He spoke a few harsh sentences in a Huron dialect to the six Indians. His tone was sharp and commanding, and they stood where they were for a few seconds. Then the man in the red jacket spoke up harshly. He said only a few words before Brant cut him off with another sharp command. The Missisaugas looked at each other, then turned as one man and loped away, heading back the way they had come.

"It's well we were here, David," Brant said. "They would have killed you."

"Now, David," Isaac said with a smile, "we are on even

terms again. You saved my life, and my father and I have saved yours."

Dave stared at them helplessly, unable to speak.

"Come into the fort," Brant said, laughing. "We have food and a warm fire."

CHAPTER NINETEEN

"You didn't know that Fort Stanwix had been abandoned?" Brant asked when they were seated around a bright fire just inside the gate.

Dave shook his head. He held a piece of deer meat in his hands, given him by Isaac, but even his great hunger wasn't enough to overcome his overwhelming sense of failure. All this way, and now to be forced to return to Niagara! It was too much to bear. He felt like crying.

Sam was at the moment unconcerned with the future; he was tearing noisily at a chunk of venison.

"Go ahead," Brant said with a smile. "You'd better eat something, David."

Dave asked a question before he bit into the meat. "Of all people I wouldn't expect to see at Fort Stanwix, you top the list, sir. What are you doing here?"

Brant nodded with a smile. "I told you that Isaac and I were going on a journey," the Indian said quietly. "I don't think I'll lead any more raids into the Mohawk Valley. Isaac and I will go to join my wife and my other children in Canada. My people will never return to the land of their forefathers, but I wanted my son to see it once again. I wanted to see it myself. So we are on our way to the Mohawk Valley."

His voice changed as bitterness entered it. "We will sneak through the hills like criminals, shunning every human we may see. We will lie on our bellies on the ridges, looking down at the places where our towns used to be. We will look at the fields and the forests and the river. I will tell Isaac of the old days and the old ways of the Mohawks, when we had power and wealth and pride. I will tell him how mighty a nation we were. When we have remained hidden in our homeland for a few days, admiring its beauty, we will turn our backs upon it and return to Canada. This is our last visit home."

"It's a dangerous trip for just two men to make," Dave ventured.

"They've tried to catch me before, David. They won't do it this time."

What will he do with us? Dave wondered. He'll have to change his plans now that he has us to deal with.

"I suppose you two ran away from Captain Millard?" Brant asked.

Dave nodded. He couldn't speak with his mouth full of meat.

"And you sought the safety of Stanwix, not knowing that the rebels had withdrawn their troops to the valley?"

"That's right," Dave said.

"We met those Missisaugas yesterday," Brant said. "They'd just left this place then. I'm surprised they didn't burn it. There's nothing pleases them more than a big bonfire. It's fortunate for you two that Isaac and I hadn't started east this morning."

"Thanks for saving us," Dave said. "I wish I could say it better."

"That's good enough. We have owed it to you since the time of the bear. And now you wonder what will become of you, don't you?"

Dave nodded.

"You thought you were finally free, and now you are captives again," Brant said.

"Druther be a captive than dead," Sam grunted, speaking across the bone he was gnawing.

Brant pushed himself to his feet and paced up and down before the three young men. "What do you think we should do with them, Isaac?"

The young Indian grinned. "Take them with us to Canada and hold them until their people pay a fortune for them."

Brant smiled back. "They aren't worth much in their present state."

Brant turned his eyes steadily on Dave. "I have said that we go to Canada to stay, David. I don't suppose you'd want to reconsider and come with us to make your home there?"

"No, sir," Dave said. "You know I wouldn't."

Brant nodded. "I know it. You want to go home to enjoy the victory and the new country you are making. I understand. So that leaves my son and me with the problem of taking two prisoners with us on a journey into the enemy's country, where there will be danger at all times. What should we do about it?"

He answered his own question, smiling broadly. "We'll take you and the other young man with us, David. You might meet more Missisaugas. And when the time comes, you will go your way and we will go ours. You will be free to go home, you and young Hawkins."

Sam Hawkins dropped his bone and stared in amazement at Brant. "You mean you're going to turn us loose?"

Brant nodded. "On one condition," he said.

"What is that, sir?" Dave asked, eager to agree to any terms that would mean freedom.

"You must give your word that you will tell no one in the valley that Isaac and I are roaming around the hills. I don't care to be shot now that there is no longer any reason for it."

"We won't tell a livin' soul, will we, Dave?" Sam said quickly.

Dave shook his head. "We won't tell anybody, sir."

"All right, then," Brant replied. "Let us go on together."

It was two days before they reached the German Flats. They stood on a wooded rise north of the river, looking at the brown, stubbled fields of the bottom lands, dotted here and there by black patches that marked the charred remains of houses and barns. In the distance was the log palisade of Fort Herkimer, one of the string of frontier forts that had defied Brant and his Indians and the Butlers and their Rangers throughout the long border war. They had burned and pillaged a thousand miles of the border, but had never made a successful assault on one of these forts, although several in Pennsylvania's Wyoming Valley had surrendered to them. Brant had once described the forts, in a letter to the commandant at Niagara, as woodchuck holes "into which they scurry at the first sign of danger."

Now he pointed to Fort Herkimer. "There you are," he said to Dave and Sam. "Walk down and tell them to let you in." He smiled grimly as he surveyed their buckskin clothing, so evidently Indian in workmanship. "Tell them who you are while you are still out of musket range. They're apt to be nervous about strangers."

"If they shoot at you, come back," Isaac said with a laugh. "You can be *sure* that we are your friends."

Joseph Brant smiled and shook his head. "Just call out before you get too close. You'll be all right. They're your people." He paused. "So the time has come."

Dave nodded. "I guess it has."

In the few brief seconds that he and Brant looked steadily at each other, memories of those past months crowded into his mind.

There were things he would never experience again, he told himself. He could hear the incessant rolling thunder of Niagara. He could see the vast panorama of the fort and the temporary city built around it: the Indian children and the omnipresent dogs darting among the houses, the brilliant precision of redcoats on parade, the bright blue sea of Ontario stretching to the horizon, the military neatness of the Ranger barracks across the river. He remembered the quiet friendliness of Miss Molly, the pleasure of working with Dan Millard and his pretty Indian wife, and Catherine Dochstadter's dark eyes laughing at him.

Most of all, he told himself, he would never forget Brant talking of his people and their traditions, his resonant voice in the dusk speaking of glories that were gone forever, a great man pouring his life into the fierce struggle to bring back those glories in the twilight hours of his race, knowing even while he fought so fiercely and valiantly that he and his people were doomed to defeat.

He thought again of the eagle to which he had likened Brant—proud and powerful and invincible in combat, but sure to suffer the same destiny that awaited the eagle— retreating forever before the white man's civilization.

"You had better go now," Brant said. "There may be hunting parties in the hills. It isn't safe for us to be here." He stepped forward to Dave. "Let us shake hands in the white man's fashion, David. I hope that the time you spent with us will be a good memory in the years ahead."

"I was just thinking that it would, sir," Dave answered. "I thank you for all that you did for me."

They shook hands and stepped apart. Sam came forward with a solemn air to shake hands with Brant.

Isaac smiled sadly and put his hand on Dave's shoulder. He spoke in Mohawk. "We met as enemies, but we part as friends. Good-by, David."

"Good-by, Isaac," Dave answered, holding out his hand.

The two young men started down the slope. Brant called after them, "God keep you both in health and happy ways."

Dave looked around and waved. "Thank you, sir."

Brant seemed about to speak again. Dave waited, looking back. But the Indian only smiled at him once more and lifted his hand in farewell.

Dave and Sam started down the hill again. When next they looked back, Brant and his son had vanished into the forest.

CHAPTER TWENTY

It was almost sunset when they approached the fort. The gates had already been closed for the night. Dave and Sam stopped walking on the plain, well outside accurate musket range. "Hello, the fort!" Dave called. "Can you open the gates and let us in?"

"Gates are closed," a suspicious voice answered faintly. "Ain't nobody gettin' in till mornin'."

"We're friends," Sam yelled. "Continental soldiers."

"Who are ye?" the voice asked.

"Harper and Hawkins," Dave answered. "Captured in March at Fort Stanwix. We've just come from the Indian country—from Niagara."

There was silence for a while, as if the sentries were conferring.

"The durn fools!" Sam said impatiently. "Why don't they let us in? What harm can two men do?"

"The whole corps of Rangers might be behind us, waiting for 'em to open the gate," Dave said. "They're doing the right thing, Sam."

"Harper!" the voice in the fort called. "Are you Nat Harper's son David?"

"That's right," Dave answered.

"Jest a minute, Harper!"

After another brief delay a sally port in the main gate swung open. A man dressed in buckskins stepped through and came toward them with the long graceful stride of a woodsrunner. As soon as the man was out of the shadow of the palisade and could be seen in the fading sunlight, Dave recognized John Bean, an old friend of his father. Bean had been a trapper and pothunter for Mohawk Valley towns until the war came and then had served three years with Morgan's riflemen. He had returned to the Mohawk country to scout for Colonel Willett.

Dave pumped Bean's hand when the tall scout came up. "Good to see you, Johnny." Dave grinned. "It sure is."

"I guess you're glad to see anybody human after all them Injuns," Bean said. "You run off from 'em?"

"That's right," Dave said. "Have you seen my family, Johnny?"

"Seen 'em durin' the summer. I made a swing over to Schoharie and down to Oghquaga, lookin' for stray Injuns. They was all fine then, Dave. Yore ma will be glad to see you, I can tell you. Likely she'll cry her eyes out."

"How are the boys? They're growing up, I'll bet."

"They're bigger than they was last time you seen 'em," Bean agreed. "Bein' with the Injuns has stretched you some too. Who is this young feller?"

Dave introduced Sam, who shook Bean's hand heartily.

Bean leaned on the barrel of his long rifle and looked them up and down with a toothy grin on his long face. "You look like you hit every bramble patch between here and Niagara. How'd you boys get away?"

Dave told how they had escaped from the party return-ing to Niagara, and he described the race to Stanwix and their pursuit by the Missisaugas but said nothing about Joseph Brant. Bean would jump at the chance to find Joseph Brant in the Mohawk Valley.

"So," he said with a warning look at Sam, "we shook the Indians near Fort Stanwix and then came here as fast as we could."

Bean eyed him searchingly, his keen blue eyes holding Dave's gaze. "Surprise you, did it, to find nobody at Stanwix?"

"It sure did," Sam blurted out. "We come runnin' up, and the place was empty."

Bean grinned. "Runnin', eh? With them Canadian Injuns right behind you. How'd you say you shook 'em?"

Sam tried to repair his error. "I guess we could run faster'n they could."

"Pretty fast runner, ain't you?" Bean said quietly. "Ain't many men can run clean off from six Injuns."

The men in the fort were impatient. "Bean! Come on in. We got to lock the gate."

"Let's go," Bean said, turning toward the gate. "Dave, I'd like to see the look on your ma's face when she sees you. She heard you was taken, but nothin' since. Truth to tell, everybody thought you was dead."

They approached the sally port, where a curious crowd was waiting. Dave could no longer keep from asking about Hannah's whereabouts. He touched Bean's arm and received an inquiring look. "What is it, Dave?"

Dave hesitated. "Johnny, we didn't know Stanwix was abandoned until we got there. Do you know where the folks went that were there?"

Bean shrugged his shoulders. "Some of the troops is here

in the valley, and some went on to Albany and down-river, I guess."

"There was a woman kept store in Stanwix. Her name was Armstrong. I thought maybe her daughter left word for me. Girl with red hair."

"That pretty one that was took by Dochstadter and his bunch last summer? I remember her. Ain't seen her, Dave, since she was took."

"Did the civilians from Stanwix come through here, Johnny?"

"Sure did," Bean answered. "No other way for 'em to go, is there? I remember the girl's mother, Dave. She come through with a new husband. One of the officers from the fort. They was on their way to his home. Seems to me it was one of them towns in the Hudson Valley. Peekskill or Newburgh or Fishkill. One of them towns."

"Which one, Johnny? Can't you even remember which one?"

"No reason to remember it. I didn't know neither of 'em. I'm sorry, Dave."

"All right, Johnny. I'll find out."

Inside the fort, Johnny Bean took the two young men to his own quarters, a tiny hut built against the palisade. The curious crowd pressed around until Dave and Sam went into the hut, then went about its business. After five years of border warfare, there was no longer any sustained interest in the return of captives from the Indian country.

When John Bean had put some chunks on the fire and had lit a couple of candles, Sam spoke of the subject that was first in his mind. "You suppose we could have some food, Mr. Bean? I could eat a horse in three bites without stoppin' to chew."

"We ain't got no horses, Sam," Bean said equably, rummaging in a cabinet near the fireplace. "I've got a couple of cold partridge here you can start on, and I'll have some deer meat ready by the time you pick the bones."

While they ate, Bean talked about affairs in the valley and the progress of the war. Dave expected that the tall woodsman would bring up the subject of the escape from the Missisaugas. Obviously Bean knew he hadn't received the entire story, but it wasn't mentioned again.

"Did they get the news out to Niagara?" Bean asked. "I mean about Cornwallis givin' up in Virginia."

"We heard it, Johnny, just before we came away. Brant and Millard think the people in London are through sending armies over here."

Bean laughed. "They better be! We got the war won right now, even if the fightin' lasts a while longer. You heard about Walter Butler?"

"We did, Johnny. Were you there?"

Bean nodded grimly. "I was right there, Dave. At Johnstown when we started 'em runnin', then in the chase through the storm when the wolves was howlin' around 'em, and when we caught up with 'em at the Canada Creek. I was with the Oneidas on the near bank when they was shootin' at Walter Butler. Some soldiers was shootin' at him too. They all claim they killed him. They think it's somethin' to brag on." Bean shook his head. "I could of put a ball in him, but I didn't. I just stood there watchin' him on his horse, right out there in the open with the bullets flyin' all around him. I never had no use for him either."

"Colonel Butler took it hard, Johnny."

"Likely he did. Well, I knew 'em both before the war, them and Brant and the Johnsons. I can't take it in my heart to be sorry. Walter Butler had his choice—King or Congress, like the rest of us."

"Captain Butler wasn't as bad as folks make out, Johnny. Most of the loyalists out there are just like other people."

Bean eyed Dave with a questioning smile. "You don't call 'em Tories any more? Loyalists, eh? I expect you been talkin' too much to Joseph Brant, Dave. I'll tell you this. Black ain't white, nor the other way around. You heard one thing from Brant, and you'll hear the other side from now on. Maybe the truth of it lies somewheres right in the middle."

Dave answered heatedly, "If it hadn't been for Brant, Johnny, we——" He broke off, realizing that he was about to tell Bean how they'd escaped from the Missisaugas.

Bean laughed. "Go ahead and say it. I got an idea what it is."

Sam interrupted. "What's goin' to happen to me and Dave now? We're still in the army, ain't we? Will they let us go home for a time?"

"They'd ought to give you leave to see your folks. See about it in the mornin'. I'll put in a word for you. Dave said you come from Kingston, didn't he? That where you learned how to run so fast?"

Sam flushed but didn't answer. Bean laughed loudly. "I guess you'll tell me when you get ready," he said. "Sam, you can get through the mountains this time o' year. You go with Dave to Schoharie and then on across to Kingston. I'll get you a couple horses in the mornin'."

"That sure will be fine," Sam answered. "That deer meat ready yet?"

"Just about," Bean said, turning to the fireplace to check the sizzling venison steaks that dangled on a spit over the fire. "Kingston," he said musingly. "Maybe that was the place that Mrs. Armstrong and her new husband was goin' to. Wish I could remember for you, Dave."

"I'll find out," Dave said.

"I expect you will," Bean said. "A man will chase a pretty girl a long ways when he's young like you fellers. Get a little older, you wait for 'em to come to you."

In the morning, with Bean's help, they arranged furloughs for a month. Bean managed to borrow two horses for the trip. Their departure was interrupted by a flurry of excitement at the gate. A bearded scout in buckskins was talking to the sentries, one of whom went running for an officer.

"That's Will Heintzleman," Bean told the young men. "He went out huntin' yesterday. Somethin's up. Let's go see."

Dave and Sam led their saddled horses to the gate, arriving in time to hear Heintzleman say, "I'm sure the big one was Brant. I seen him lots o' times. The other was only a young feller. But I know Brant. It was him, all right."

"What's all this, Will?" Bean asked the scout.

"I jumped two Injuns this mornin'. They was camped up in the hills. I was on a deer run, still-huntin'. I come up to maybe eight yards of 'em when they pulled foot. I only had one shot at 'em."

"You say it was Brant?" Bean asked mildly, looking at Dave.

"It sure was, Johnny. Let's you and me and some of the boys go after him."

"My friend Dave Harper here just came through the Injun country, Will. Brant was at Oswego when Dave left. Wasn't he, Dave?"

"That's right, Johnny. When Sam and I escaped, Brant was at Oswego."

"These boys know what they're talkin' about, Will. They run clean off from six Canadian Injuns yestiddy. Didn't you, fellers?"

Dave looked at Bean's grinning face. "That's right. We did."

"And you don't want to tell all the little odds and ends about it, do you, fellers?"

"No," Dave said quietly. "We can't tell them all."

"That's what I figgered," Bean said.

"What's all this about?" Heintzleman said angrily. "I'm talkin' about Joseph Brant, and you're gabbin' about some Canadian Injuns. I'm tellin' you, Johnny, Brant is up in them hills. My eyes is just as good as they always was."

An officer came running up, and Heintzleman told his story again. The officer nodded excitedly when Heintzleman suggested that a scouting party go out immediately.

"Now, hold on, Capt'n," Johnny Bean said mildly. "You don't want to send the men out to chase two Oneidas who was huntin' the same deer that Will was after."

"If they was Oneidas," Heintzleman said heatedly, "what'd they run for? I never took a shot at no Oneida in my life. The feller I let fly at was the big Injun hisself, Joseph Brant!"

"Dave Harper says Brant was at Oswego, Capt'n," Bean insisted. "Dave ain't a liar."

"No reason Brant couldn't of come down here," Heintzleman cried. "Them two fellers made it. He could of too. Let's quit wastin' time and go after 'im."

"What'd he come for, Will? Without a war party. Admit you're wrong. You seen two Oneidas."

"Why did they run?" Heintzleman asked again. "What's the matter with you, Johnny? You know I wouldn't take Brant for any Oneida that ever lived."

"I'd run too, Will, if you was bangin' at me with that rifle."

"Bean's right, Heintzleman," the officer said finally. "Brant wouldn't come into the valley without two or three hundred Injuns. He never has. And it's too late in the season for war parties."

Heintzleman kept talking, but nobody believed him. A few minutes later he stalked angrily away, muttering to himself that he knew Joseph Brant when he saw him, and there wasn't a man in the world was goin' to tell him different.

Bean walked out of Fort Herkimer with the two young men. They mounted their horses while Bean looked up at them, grinning. "So you ain't such a fast runner, after all, are you, young Hawkins?"

Sam shrugged and smiled.

"We promised Brant we wouldn't tell he was in the valley," Dave said. "The young Indian is his son. They just wanted to take a last look at the valley. They know they're never coming back. We had to keep our promise, Johnny."

"It's safe with me, Dave. Let him take his last look and then good riddance to him. I'll keep Will Heintzleman off him. You go on home to your folks."

"Thanks for all you've done, Johnny."

Bean grinned and waved them off. They turned the horses on the long road to Schenectady.

The following afternoon as they rode through rolling farmland, Dave pointed out to Sam his uncle's farm. It was within sight of the Middle Fort, one of the three stockades in the Schoharie Valley.

"You go on ahead, Dave. I'll come a little slower."

Dave hooked his heels into his horse's flanks, and the startled animal galloped along the wagon road. Dave saw his two brothers sawing wood alongside the barn. They stopped working when they heard the horse. Dave waved his arm and yelled, but he was too far away for them to recognize him. They stood watching his approach. Suddenly they started to run for the road.

Dave saw a woman come to the doorway of the house and stand there, shading her eyes against the sun. Then she turned, called into the house, and began to run after the boys.

"Ma!" Dave yelled. "It's me, Dave! I've come home."

He jumped from the horse when he reached them, and for the next minute he was alternately kissing his mother and pounding his brothers. They were all laughing and shouting greetings. Mrs. Harper kept dabbing her eyes with her apron.

It was some time before the boys quieted enough for Dave to hear what his mother was saying. She was tugging his arm and telling him there was somebody waiting for him at the house. He looked that way.

Hannah stood in the open doorway, smiling at him. His heart leaped. He took a couple of slow steps forward and then started to run. She came forward to meet him. His arms went around her and they held each other closely. He kissed her while his brothers shouted with glee.

"I promised I'd be waiting, Dave," she said.

"I've been worried sick ever since we found Stanwix empty."

"No more worrying, Dave," she said, looking up with a joyful smile. "Never again."

"Maybe I better ask you now, Hannah. I've been long enough getting to it. Will you marry me?"

"What do you think I'm here for, Dave?" she whispered as his arms tightened around her.